Dear Reader,

Welcome back to Sunrise Key—home to billion-aire Preston Seaholm and his posh four-star beach resort, and the setting for *Otherwise Engaged*.

I've always been a beach person. As a kid, my family vacationed each summer on the Jersey Shore, and I quickly came to love the sound of the surf and the fresh ocean air. A few years back, I discovered Florida's beautiful Gulf Coast, and now I am fortunate enough to be able to spend half of each year living on a little island off Sarasota, not unlike Sunrise Key.

But back when I wrote my Sunrise Key trilogy, that was just one of my dreams—to live within a bike ride of the sparkling Gulf of Mexico, to feel the fine white sand beneath my feet, to live among palm trees and tropical birds. . . .

It was a dream I passed along—and granted—to Molly Cassidy, the heroine of *Otherwise Engaged*, when she unexpectedly inherits the Kirk Estate, a crumbling old beachfront mansion—a piece of property that is high on Preston Seaholm's "must acquire" list.

But then Pres meets Molly and her ten-year-old son, and his entire world gets turned upside down as he finally learns that all of his money can't buy him what he really longs to acquire: true love and happiness.

If you enjoy this visit to Sunrise Key, look for my other books in the Sunrise Key trilogy. *Kiss and Tell* (Leila and Marsh's story) and *The Kissing Game* (Francine and Simon's story) are both available, also from Bantam Books, at a bookstore near you!

Welcome back to Sunrise Key! I hope you'll visit often!

Love,

Suzanne Brockmann

Suz

OTHER TITLES BY
SUZANNE BROCKMANN

Hot Pursuit
Into the Fire
Dark of Night
All Through the Night
Force of Nature
Forbidden
Into the Storm
Ladies' Man
Heartthrob
Bodyguard
The Unsung Hero
The Defiant Hero
Over the Edge
Out of Control
Into the Night
Gone Too Far
Flashpoint
Hot Target
Breaking Point
Freedom's Price
Body Language
Kiss and Tell
The Kissing Game

SUZANNE BROCKMANN

~

Otherwise Engaged

BANTAM BOOKS

2009 Bantam Books Mass Market Edition

Copyright © 1997 by Suzanne Brockmann

Published in the United States by Bantam Books, an imprint of The Random House Publishing Group, a division of Random House, Inc., New York.

BANTAM BOOKS and the rooster colophon are registered trademarks of Random House, Inc.

Originally published in mass market in the United States by Bantam Books, a division of Random House, Inc., in 1997.

ISBN 978-0-553-59251-1

Cover design: Lynn Andreozzi
Cover art: Alan Ayers

Printed in the United States of America

www.bantamdell.com

9 8 7 6 5 4 3 2 1

For my very patient family and friends

ACKNOWLEDGMENTS

My grateful thanks to Jay Gravina for sharing his scuba-diving expertise, and to my son, Jason, for giving me firsthand experience both with unique and wonderful ten-year-old boys and with hearing impairment. Also thanks to my Mission Impossible Team: Jodie, Bill, Deede, Ed, Mel, Jace, Carolee, and especially Patricia.

ONE

IT WAS GOING to rain.

Molly Cassidy knew without a doubt that it was going to pour buckets from the huge dark clouds that were looming over the Gulf of Mexico and moving steadily closer.

Last night it had rained just a little and the roof of this enormous, white stucco Spanish eclectic-style house that she and Zander had inherited had done a fine imitation of a sieve.

Molly had bought tarps first thing that morning, but in this wind, tying the last of them over the low-pitched, rambling red-tiled roof was proving to be a two-person job.

Lightning cracked in the distance, and the boom of thunder was quick to follow. Instinctively, she flattened herself on the roof, the hair on the back of her neck rising. Was she nuts? On the roof during an electrical storm?

But this decaying, moldy, wonderful old architectural monster was their future. It was their chance at a new beginning, a fresh, clean start.

And it would be much more fresh and clean if there weren't two inches of water standing in the living room by nightfall.

As another rumble of thunder rolled, Molly lifted her head and peered over the crest of the roof down toward the ground. She could see her ten-year-old son looking up at her, his thin face pinched with concern, his eyes huge behind his glasses. Zander hated thunder and lightning. He always had, even as a baby.

"Get down from there," he signed up at her, his hands moving swiftly, sharply. "Now."

"Go inside," Molly signed back. "I'm almost done."

"Hurry!"

"Go inside," Molly signed again. "Make sure all the windows are closed. Quickly!"

Zander turned and dashed inside, and Molly looked down at the tarp, wondering the best way to untangle it in this wind with only two hands. Maybe she should just tie it down the way it was. It would be better than nothing. . . .

But then the wind rose and the tarp whipped up and over her, covering her and nearly knocking her off the roof. She slid, cursing and scrambling for a finger- or toehold on the slippery mission tile.

Her foot hit a loose tile and caught just as strong hands grabbed her around the waist and hauled her against a hard body. Who the heck. . . ?

Molly pushed the tarp off her head and found herself nose-to-nose with the Beach Boy.

She'd seen him out on the beach every morning since they'd first arrived on Sunrise Key three days before. He had an artist's easel and watercolor paints and he always sat quietly in the early-morning light, painting the changing colors of the ocean.

A surprising number of people were on the

beach early in the morning, but there was something about this man that had caught her eye.

It was more than his gleaming, golden-tanned, beach-boy good looks. Even though everything about him seemed to glisten—his sun-bleached, reddish-gold hair, his trim, muscular, tan body— Molly refused to allow herself to be impressed by a handsome face. But this man had a certain air about him. And it was that, she told herself, his calm authority, that had drawn her attention to him. Of course, once her attention had been caught, she couldn't help but notice that movie-star face and extremely well-maintained body.

Molly had never gotten close enough to see if his paintings were any good.

Or if his eyes were as brilliantly blue as she'd imagined.

They weren't. They were hazel. How refreshing.

"You all right?" he asked, his voice a raspy baritone flavored with a hint of the South. He was a smoker—the lingering scent of cigarette smoke clung to him.

Molly nodded, wide-eyed, aware that his arms were still around her, aware of his leg thrown across hers in his attempt to hold her in place, aware of the heat of his skin against hers.

She was anchored.

Up close, he wasn't as perfectly good-looking as she'd thought. His face was harder, leaner, his nose sharper and slightly crooked, and a small scar marred his left cheekbone, underneath his eye. He hadn't shaved in a number of days, and his scruffy chin glinted with shades of red and gold, making him look less like a beach boy and more like a pirate. And those eyes...

They were the color of the ocean as the storm clouds approached, green and gray and darkly dangerous.

"Come on," he said, his voice nearly inaudible over the rising wind. "I'll help you. You get this side, I'll take the other."

Molly nodded again, and just like that, his weight was off her, the intimate warmth of his bare leg against hers was gone.

He was up and over to the other side of the roof as if he were a professional tightrope walker, escaped from the Ringling Circus Museum in Sarasota, several dozens of miles up the Florida coastline. As he went he untangled and smoothed down the tarp. The muscles in his arms tightened as a big gust tried to whip the blue plastic away from him, and he brought his weight down, holding the tarp with his body against the roof.

His thick, gorgeous hair was pushed forward into his eyes and then quickly dashed back out by the rising wind. He ignored it, lashing the rope at the tarp's corner securely into place.

Molly did the same on her end. It wasn't perfect, but it was much better than nothing.

Lightning streaked across the sky and thunder boomed. And the heavens opened, showering them with big, fat raindrops that fell faster and faster until there was only a sheet of water, pouring down from the clouds.

Thunder cracked again, deafeningly loud. Molly could see the Beach Boy crouched by the ladder, chivalrously waiting for her to descend first.

She skidded on the plastic, and he reached for her, his hand around her wrist holding her steady. Their eyes met, and he smiled, a quick, fierce, genuine smile that electrified and heated his gaze.

He was having fun. He actually *liked* being up on the roof in the middle of a thunderstorm, with the wind and the rain ripping at his clothes and his hair, danger all around him.

Molly scrambled down the ladder and dashed toward the shelter of the house. The Beach Boy was right behind her.

Zander was inside, waiting. The roar of the wind and the rain was quieted as Molly shut the door behind them.

"Oh, *man*," Molly gasped.

"Welcome to Florida." The Beach Boy was still grinning at her.

He was dripping wet. His hair was plastered against his head, and his eyelashes were beaded with drops of water. But his smile was infectious, and Molly found herself smiling back at him.

The Beach Boy looked down at the puddle he was making on the marble-tiled floor. His T-shirt and cutoff jeans were soaked, as were the ragged boat sneakers he wore without socks. "So much for keeping the rain outside," he said ruefully.

Zander was staring, blue eyes wide behind his glasses. "Who is he?" he signed to Molly, using small furtive movements. It was the American Sign Language equivalent of whispering, and it wasn't very polite.

"Please run and get us a couple of towels," Molly told her son, signing the word *towels* for emphasis, and the boy dashed away.

But *who is he?* was a very good question indeed. She turned to the Beach Boy. "Thank you so much," Molly said to him.

He was staring off after Zander. "Is your boy deaf?" he asked, turning to gaze at her with those odd-colored eyes. "I didn't realize...."

Others might have been put off by the bluntness of his question, but Molly liked it. It was so much better than what most people did—staring askance at the boy's hearing aids and then ignoring both the child and his physical challenge.

"Zander's hearing-impaired."

"Zander?" One golden eyebrow lifted, and the start of another smile danced on the edges of his lips.

"It's short for Alexander. He's got a severe high-frequency hearing loss—and high frequency is where most of human speech occurs. His hearing aids make up for some of that, but not all. If you speak clearly and let him watch your lips, he'll understand most of what you say. And what he doesn't understand, he'll ask about. He's not shy."

The Beach Boy nodded, his disturbingly warm gaze searching her face. "He looks just like you. It's very cool—it's like you should be put on display with a big sign that says 'Genetics in Action.'"

Molly couldn't help but laugh at that. "Well, I think he's the most gorgeous, perfect child in the world, so thank you very much." She looked up to see Zander reappear with the towels. He handed them both to her.

She gave one to the man. "Thanks," he said, including Zander with a look and a nod.

Molly opened her own towel, wiped her face, and blotted her hair. "I'm Molly Cassidy," she told him.

"I know that. Me and everyone else on the island. It's a pretty small place, you know—and news travels faster than the speed of light down here."

"I've seen you on the beach," Molly said.

"Yeah, I'm trying to learn to paint." He smiled, but didn't offer her his name. It was odd—as if he assumed she already knew him. "You know, this

old house has been leaking for at least fifty years."
He wrung out the edge of his T-shirt. "Why'd you
choose today to break tradition?"

Molly peered out at him from under her towel.
"Because I intend to make this place into a bed-
and-breakfast—and soaked mattresses and soggy
toast is *not* what I have in mind."

"A B-and-B, huh? That's a lot of hard work."

Not compared with what she'd been used to.
But Molly just smiled, kicking off her saturated
sneakers.

The Beach Boy looked at her son. "How about
you, Zander? You want to make this place into a
B-and-B?"

"I like it here," Zander said. "I want to stay."

"We like the idea of working for ourselves."
Molly pulled the ponytail holder from her wet
hair and ran her hands through the light brown
tangle.

"Why not sell the place?" the man asked, his
eyes following the movement of her fingers. "An
old building like this, with all this property? You
could name your price, walk away with a pile of
cash. And if you invested it right, you wouldn't
have to work at all."

"*Invest* it? No thank you very much." Molly made the sign of the cross with her fingers, holding it up as if to ward him off. "Been there, done that. At least my husband did. And it's not a mistake I'm going to make twice."

"You could find some low-risk—"

"Risk is risk," she interrupted. "No, I'll stick to what I know, thanks."

"You could find someone who *does* know to invest the money for you."

Molly laughed. "Here comes the part where you introduce yourself and tell us that when you're not vacationing here on Sunrise Key, you work in New York City managing people's investments, right?" She started for the stairs to the second floor, turning back to face Zander. "We better check our buckets, Z—see where we're still leaking." She smiled at the Beach Boy. "Come on, Mr. Investment Banker, tag along. We'll give you the official leaky-roof tour of the Kirk Estate."

He started up the stairs after them. "I'm not an investment banker," he said. "I'm sorry I didn't introduce myself—I thought you knew who I was."

"Oh, wait a minute, *I* know who you are,"

Molly teased, checking the buckets that were strategically placed across the upstairs landing. Several places were dripping, but it wasn't the steady stream of water she'd expected without the tarps. "You're the island's famous billionaire, Preston Seaholm the third, or whatever pretentious number he has dangling off the end of his name, right? You've come to make your fifth offer for this house—" She turned to face him. "Can you *believe* the nerve of that pompous man? He's made four offers on a house that's not even for sale in the course of three days. Isn't that incredibly crass! Zander—please check the buckets in your room, and the other bedrooms on that side of the hall, okay?" She signed "check the buckets please" for emphasis.

As Zander disappeared down the corridor Molly pushed open the door to the room she'd slept in over the past few nights. Last night, she'd woken up with water dripping onto her nose. She'd moved the bed and wound up directly underneath another leak. She'd ended up putting buckets and plastic containers on the bed, and taking her blanket and pillow down to the couch in the den.

"He must really want to buy this place," the Beach Boy said, following her and continuing their conversation.

"Who? Preston Seaholm the fifth?" Molly snorted. "You know, for all he knows, we're in mourning for poor Great-Uncle Jeremiah Kirk. And all he wants to talk about is money. I know his type. Egotistical, overbearing, thinks he owns the world—"

"*Are* you in mourning?"

Molly led the way into another bedroom. "Well, no. We didn't exactly even know of Jeremiah's existence until two weeks ago when the lawyer contacted us about his death. He was my husband's great-uncle. I didn't even know Chuck—my husband—had other surviving family."

"Don't you think that Pres Seaholm probably knows your connection to Jeremiah Kirk was distant? I mean, if he wants to buy this place that badly..."

The room Molly thought of as the lavender bedroom had a drip that was running pretty quickly. She turned to search for the largest, widest container, but the Beach Boy beat her to it, already switching it with the small plastic bowl that had been under the leak.

His hair was starting to dry, and the red highlights gleamed in the dim light. And it *was* dim in there. Molly was positive there were no lightbulbs stronger than forty watts in the entire house. It made it difficult to read at night, but the glow they cast was warm and intimate and filled with interesting shadows.

It was romantic.

Of course, this guy would cut a romantic enough figure even in the glaring light of high noon. But with the storm raging outside, turning the afternoon unnaturally dark, in these still-unfamiliar rooms, filled with furniture that was nearly three times as old as she was, Molly was suddenly painfully aware that the man she was talking to was among the most attractive of all the men she'd ever met.

Including Chuck.

She shook her head, pushing that errant thought away.

"Have I thanked you properly for saving my life up on the roof?" she asked.

"That depends on what you mean by *properly*."

His gaze dropped to her mouth for just a fraction of a second, but it was long enough for Molly to realize that he found her attractive too. He wanted to kiss her. She remembered the sensation of his leg thrown across hers, of his hard body pressed against hers. She was willing to bet he remembered it too.

If she kissed him, he would probably taste like an ashtray.

That should have been enough of a turnoff for a pro–fresh air nonsmoker like herself, but oddly enough it wasn't.

She turned away, uncertain of whether she was more afraid of him or her reaction to him, and unable to keep from glancing back in his direction.

He was smiling as if he could read her mind. She didn't doubt that he could. "You said your husband was Chuck—Chuck Cassidy...? Do you mean the writer?"

She gazed at him in surprise. "Did you know him?"

"No, but I've read all of his books. He was a favorite of mine. I think his short story 'Day After the End' is still required reading in ninth-grade English in most of the western hemisphere. As it should be." His voice got lower. "I was sorry to hear of his death."

With the exception of "Day After the End," by the time Chuck had died, his name and his books were virtually unknown. He'd published nothing since 1979—more than five years before Molly had even met him. Writing had always been a struggle for him, and in the last years of his life he'd fought, but not nearly hard enough. And then, when he was diagnosed with cancer...

"That was about two years ago, wasn't it?" he asked.

"Three," Molly said. "I'm surprised you even knew. Chuck Cassidy's passing wasn't exactly considered newsworthy."

"His obituary was in the local paper."

She blinked. "Here? On Sunrise Key?"

"Yeah. According to local legend, he used to come down here for vacations all the time, back fifteen, twenty years ago. He even lived down here for a while. It was before I came to the key, but there's still a picture of him up on the wall at Millie's Market."

Molly turned away. "I didn't know." It was amazing. Another secret. Another piece of himself that Chuck hadn't shared with her. He'd never told her anything about Sunrise Key, Florida.

But then again, Chuck hadn't told her much about *any*thing.

The Beach Boy was watching her and she forced herself to smile.

And change the subject. "So, what is it?" she asked him. "Mike? Or Tom?"

T W O

He blinked. "Excuse me?"

"Your name," Molly said. "No, don't tell me. It's Brian, right?"

His name. She honest to God didn't know who he was. Well, of course she didn't—she wouldn't have insulted him right and left if she'd known.

Not that he felt insulted. On the contrary. He was amused by her vehemence. What had she called him? Pompous. He didn't think he'd ever been called pompous before. Certainly never to his face, and probably never even behind his back. Overbearing. He didn't *think* he was overbearing—not the way some of his classmates at Harvard had been. He was intensely aggressive at times, yes, but never overbearing. And as for egotistical. Well...Perhaps she wasn't quite off base there, since it was maybe a *little* egotistical to assume that Molly Cassidy would automatically know who he was.

But on the other hand, he'd known exactly who she was the first time he saw her.

"So am I right?" She was smiling at him as she led the way back into the hall.

He followed her. Right about what? Then he remembered. His name. "Brian? Nope. Not even close."

At first glance she looked completely average. She had light brown hair, made darker now from the rain. It was a little longer than shoulder length, with a light fringe of bangs that framed her oval-shaped face.

"Pete."

He shook his head as they went down the stairs. "I honestly don't think you're going to guess."

Her nose was unremarkable, neither too big nor too small and her mouth fit nicely beneath it.

Her eyes were a very common shade of blue. She wasn't too short or too tall—just a nice, average height. She was slender, but not too skinny. Her oversized T-shirt attempted to hide her curves, but the sudden downpour of rain had drenched it, and now it did quite the opposite, clinging to her nicely proportioned body. She looked to be in her mid-twenties, but he knew she had to be older. Her boy was at least nine or ten years old.

"Steve?"

"No."

"Okay, I give up. What is your name? Bill, right?"

He laughed. "I thought you gave up."

She was a mom and a widow, and she looked the part. Wholesome. Average. Nothing special.

At first glance.

But Pres had had the opportunity to take a second glance at very, *very* close proximity up on the roof of the house.

And up close, her hair had shone with overtones of gold. It was baby-fine and soft as the purest, most expensive silk as his hands had brushed against it. Up close, her seemingly average nose had a smattering of ridiculously perfect freckles across it, and her lips looked incredibly, heart-stoppingly soft. She was quick to smile, and that smile lit her from within, transforming her and making her look anything but average.

And up close, her eyes were so much more than common. They were filled with flecks of green and gold and brown, swirling in and among an ocean that never stayed the same warm shade of blue for long.

"It's my major fault," she admitted. "I have this inability to give up. Just tell or I'll keep guessing."

He hesitated for a second or two. "My mother used to call me Michael."

"Mike—I was right the first time," she said triumphantly. "Why didn't you tell me?"

"Because most folks around here call me by my given name." He paused. "Pres Seaholm. The first."

Molly Cassidy's big blue eyes got even bigger and bluer, and Pres knew that—for the first time since they'd come down off the roof—she was about to be silent.

But her silence didn't last for long. "You're kidding, right? Please say you're only kidding."

He shook his head no, and she covered her face with her hands. "Oh, Lord."

"I wish I could tell you that I stopped by to make my fifth crass offer on the house in three days, but the truth is I was painting on the beach, taking advantage of the weird light before the storm struck."

Molly started to laugh. "Oh, Lord, I'm sorry...." She had to sit down on the stairs, she was laughing so hard. "I called you... And I said... Oh, God! You must think I'm awful."

Zander came out of his room and peered down at them over the upstairs railing. He stomped his foot, making a sharp, loud sound, and Molly glanced up. As Pres watched, the boy made some movements with his hands. It had to be sign language.

"No, I'm all right," Molly called up to her son, still laughing as she made similar motions with her hands. "I'm just..." She shook her head, turning to look at Pres. Her cheeks were flushed from embarrassment and her eyes were still brimming with laughter, making her look even younger. The effect was charming. "You're not what I expected," she said accusingly, almost as if this were all his fault.

"You mean, pompous and overbearing?" He smiled to soften his words, to make sure she knew he didn't take any of it too seriously.

She cringed, briefly closing her eyes, but didn't crumble. "You did come on way too strong," she insisted. "Making all those offers on the house like that..."

"That's not coming on too strong," he countered. "That's getting the job done. See, I want this house."

Molly stood up, and the stairs put her at eye level with him. She wasn't laughing anymore. "But it's not for sale, Mr. Seaholm. It's not even on the market."

He fished in his pocket for his cigarettes, but she stopped him before he even pulled them out.

"Yes, I mind if you smoke, so don't even ask," she told him sternly. "When I picked up the keys, I told the realtor I wasn't interested in selling. But despite that, you made an offer on the place. And I assume you talked to her—what's her name? Fox?—since she was the one who called me with your offer."

"Yeah, I talked to Maia Fox. And yeah, she told me about your conversation."

"And you made the offer anyway. Not once but *four* times. Don't you think that's maybe a little teeny tiny bit pushy?"

Pres shrugged, trying not to be daunted by the disapproval in her eyes. For some reason, it was important that she didn't dislike him. For *some* reason...? Not true. For one very *specific* reason—that he always took care to keep carefully zipped inside his pants during business deals. He had to smile at that—and at himself. It wasn't like him to think with a part of his anatomy other than his brain.

"I thought after you had a chance to see the place, to see how much work needs to be done, you'd change your mind," he told her. "And if you were going to change your mind, I didn't want to risk someone else jumping in with an offer and stealing the place out from underneath me."

She didn't look totally convinced, but his explanation at least took some of the edge off of her disapproval.

"After all," he added, "you don't get to be a

pompous, overbearing, egocentric billionaire by waiting for opportunities to find *you*."

The pink in her cheeks darkened, despite the fact that he was only teasing. "You're never going to let me live this down, are you? Damn, there goes my chance at being invited to join the Billionaires' Yacht Club," she said. "Me and my big mouth—and my foot firmly entrenched within it. Too bad—and I was *so* looking forward to the annual Sunrise Key Beach Ball Day high-society dinner dance."

"Not a problem. Sell me this house, and I'll make sure you have a pair of tickets seating you at the mayor's table."

She laughed. Pres liked making her laugh.

"Yeah, right. Big deal. There's no such thing as the annual Beach Ball Day dance."

"Sell me the house, and I'll throw one—in your honor."

"I don't get it. Is there oil on this land?" she asked, eyes narrowed. "Or maybe a gold mine underneath the basement?"

"Not that I know of."

Molly shook her head, moving past him down

the stairs. "Yeah, like you'd tell me about it if there were, right?"

The Beach Boy was Preston Seaholm, the billionaire. Lord, wasn't that just her luck.

Or maybe it *was* lucky. The Beach Boy might've turned out to be a laid-back, no-worries kind of guy who traveled with the weather and the good times and lived hand-to-mouth. He might've been the kind of guy who worked just enough to pay the rent and fill his stomach, and was available to hang around all hours of the day and night—funny and charismatic—proving to be a nuisance and a distraction.

Not to mention one hell of a temptation.

But the Beach Boy wasn't a beach boy. He was a shark—the corporate kind. He was Preston Seaholm, a man rumored to possess an unnatural need to own every available piece of property on this island, intent on making Sunrise Key his kingdom in every sense of the word.

No, she wouldn't see too much of him, thank God. No doubt his days were kept extremely full from his legendary sleeves-rolled-up, hands-on running of the Seaholm Resort, not to mention the arduous task of keeping track of all his money.

And a billion dollars would take a great deal of keeping track of.

"If there were gold or oil on this land," he told her, following her the rest of the way down to the marble-tiled front entrance, "someone would have found it already."

"So what's the big deal?" she asked. "You own everything else on the island, you don't need this place."

"Yes, I do."

"What, did you spend too much time playing Monopoly as a kid?"

He smiled. "Actually, I've never played the game."

"Went right from Candy Land to playing the stock market, huh?"

His smile turned into a grin, wide and genuinely amused. Robert Redford, Molly thought suddenly. Even though Pres Seaholm didn't look anything like Robert Redford aside from the fact that they were both men with light-colored hair and they were both breathtakingly attractive, his smile reminded her of the heartthrob actor. It was a genuine, honest smile—which either meant it *was* genuine, or like Redford, Pres Seaholm was one hell of a good actor.

"Tell me honestly, would you tease me like this if I were wearing a business suit?" he asked.

"Would you have leaped onto the roof to help me with the tarp if you were wearing a business suit?"

Preston Seaholm the first and only didn't hesitate before answering. "Yes."

She believed him. She gazed into his warm hazel eyes and...believed him. And oddly enough, she realized that she liked him. How strange. And she'd been so prepared to dislike or at least strongly disapprove of Sunrise Key's local celebrity. "You don't look like a billionaire," she admitted. "You're much younger than I thought you'd be."

"You're not what I imagined, either."

Silence surrounded them, warm and humid and suffocating. Molly couldn't seem to break away from the magnetic pull of his gaze. When she spoke, her voice was little more than a whisper. "Why *do* you want this place so badly?"

"Do you really have to ask?" He looked away from her, and Molly felt as if she'd just been released from a force field. It was all that she could do not to sag to the ground. But he was gesturing up at the second-floor landing, at the grimy chandelier above them, the intricate marble tile, and the ornate arch-shaped front door. "Look at this house," he commanded her, pushing a tumble of red-gold hair back from his forehead with a single sweep of one hand. "It's incredible."

Molly looked at the peeling paint, the mildewed wallpaper, the cheap, worn avacado-green carpeting someone had used to cover up the magnificent staircase decades ago, the dirt-streaked windows and the cracked panes of glass in the double-sash doors that led out onto a small front terrace, the chipped and filthy marble-tiled floor, one entire square replaced by cheap linoleum.

It would be an enormous task to get this place in shape, but once done, it *would* be incredible. She knew that. She could see underneath the peeling paint and the obnoxious carpeting. She could see it clean and renovated. She'd known, the very first time she'd walked into this house, that it had potential with a capital *P*. Some people might not have been able to see past the neglect, but she had.

She looked at Pres. Clearly, he was not some people. Clearly, like she had, when he looked around, he saw what could be, rather than what was.

She liked him even more for that.

"It *is* incredible," she told him. "But it's also not for sale."

He turned to face her. "There's nothing that's not for sale." He spoke the words as if they were God's eleventh commandment, accidentally left off Moses' stone tablet.

Molly crossed her arms. "Wanna bet?"

"I'll raise my last offer by a hundred thousand."

His last offer had been close to three hundred thousand dollars. That meant he was willing to pay... Molly swallowed, shaken. "You're kidding."

"I'm completely serious. I've wanted this house for years. I intend to own it."

He *was* serious. He was still smiling, but this smile didn't quite reach his eyes. The warm hazel had turned to fire from his intensity.

Molly felt bad for him. This place clearly meant a lot to this man. But it *wasn't* for sale.

She'd been so thrilled when she and Zander had arrived and they'd stared at the enormous, rambling house through the windshield of their little car. It seemed like fate had finally dealt them a winning hand.

It was as if they'd finally come home.

"I'm sorry, it's not for sale," Molly said again.

Preston Seaholm didn't say anything, didn't smile, and for the first time since she'd spotted him out on the beach with his watercolors, he actually looked like a man who might be able to write a check from his personal account for a million dollars.

He looked at her, studying her, his disconcerting eyes taking in every last detail, from the silly colorful array of nail polish she had let Zander, her budding artist, paint on her toenails, to the drooping, damp mess of her hair.

She pushed her bangs out of her eyes, self-consciously folding her arms across her chest.

"It's not for sale," he finally said, repeating her words. And then he smiled. "We'll see."

THREE

"THERE HE IS!"

Bright lights flashed on, blinding him, and Pres froze, trying to make sense of the crowd rushing toward him. There were cameras everywhere, and men and women holding microphones.

"Mr. Seaholm! Mr. Seaholm! What was your reaction, sir, to the recent announcement from the magazine . . . ?"

Mother of God, he was being descended upon by news teams. What was this about? What had he done now? He had absolutely no clue.

He spotted a microphone bearing the call letters of the local CBS affiliate, and inwardly winced. He looked like hell. He was wearing his old, worn-out painting clothes, and they were wet to boot. His hair was a mass of sodden curls, drenched again as he'd dashed from his truck to the building. Still, he stood his ground. The cameras were already rolling. They had him on tape, grunge and all. Running for cover would only make him look worse.

"Mr. Seaholm, what are your plans, sir?"

From the corner of his eye, Pres saw Dominic Defeo leading a team of security guards through the crowd—the cavalry to the rescue.

"What's this about?" he asked with as much dignity and authority as he could muster, considering he looked like a beach bum.

"*Fantasy Man* magazine," one of the reporters eagerly told him.

Fantasy Man magazine? What the hell?

"Are you going to take *Fantasy Man* magazine up on their offer?" someone asked, shoving a microphone in his face.

What offer? "I'm sorry, I'm afraid you have me at a disadvantage, I've been out of the office all day and—"

"Mr. Seaholm, do you always dress so casually on a workday?"

"Of course not. I was painting and got caught in the rain...." Normally, Pres wouldn't appear inside the resort looking the way he did. But he hadn't planned to be there for long. He'd just needed to pick up a file from his desk and collect his phone messages. And to see if Dominic—his head concierge and best friend—was free to share a beer when his shift at the front desk ended in fifteen minutes.

The truth was, Pres had wanted rather desperately to talk to someone. He wanted to talk about...what? About Molly Cassidy? About the way this little, average, wholesome mother-of-a-ten-year-old had made him feel more alive with a flash of her blue eyes than he'd felt in years?

He'd spent a small fortune bungee jumping and skydiving to feel even a third of the thrill he'd felt when he'd found himself nose-to-nose with Molly Cassidy on top of the Kirk Estate roof this afternoon.

True, the likelihood that they were both about to be fried by lightning had probably started his adrenaline flowing, but he'd felt the same heart-stopping rush when he'd looked into her eyes as they stood safe inside the foyer of the house moments later. He didn't understand it, but he liked it. He always liked an adrenaline rush.

"Mr. Seaholm, what exactly do you look for in a woman?"

Pres turned to stare at the reporter who'd asked the last question. "Excuse me?"

"Sir, are you even aware that you were voted *Fantasy Man* magazine's Most Eligible Bachelor of the Year?"

Dominic Defeo pushed his way up to the front. "I'm sorry," he said in his slightly disdainful, totally authentic-sounding, yet absolutely contrived blue-blooded Boston accent. "Mr. Seaholm doesn't have a prepared statement at this time. We'll be in touch to arrange a scheduled interview at a later date."

Pres let the concierge shepherd him back down the hall, back toward the parking lot and his pickup truck. "What the hell is going on?" he hissed through his teeth. "*Fantasy Man* magazine...?"

But Dom had on his Jeeves-the-Butler smile,

clenched teeth and all. "I'll fill you in completely in a moment, sir," he said.

The reporters were persistent, following them all the way down the hall, shouting their questions.

"Mr. Seaholm, what's your idea of a romantic evening?"

"Mr. Seaholm, what does your ex-wife have to say about all this?"

"Mr. Seaholm, do you intend to shoot the photos for the magazine in a studio, or here, on location at the resort?"

"Mr. Seaholm, is there truth to the rumor that you intend to skydive nude for the photo spread in *Fantasy Man* magazine?"

Preston stopped short and looked back at the reporters in shock. "Do I intend to do *what...*?"

"You're *Fantasy Man* magazine's Most Eligible Bachelor of the Year," Dominic told Pres as they sat in his pickup truck. Dom had slipped off both his jacket and tie and his upper-crust accent. He sat now in his shirtsleeves, his dark hair wet from the rain, and his usually world-weary brown eyes glistening with unconcealed amusement. "Congratulations."

"*Fantasy Man*," Pres echoed. "As in ... *Fantasy Man*?" He shook a cigarette free from the pack he kept rubber-banded to the sun visor and lit it with a quick snap of a match. He inhaled deeply, praying he'd somehow gotten it all wrong.

"*Fantasy Man* as in full frontal nudity, my friend." Dom's regular accent was pure Boston thug. When he was behind the front desk, he put on a gentrified act that made him seem quite a bit older than he was. But when not on the job, he didn't look much more than forty, and in reality was probably closer to Pres's own mid-thirties. "They sent a photo team down. They pulled me aside and asked my esteemed opinion as to what it would take to convince you to pose *au naturel* for a five-page spread."

Preston choked.

"Think of the publicity you could generate for this place," Dom continued. He was enjoying this much too much. "Beautiful color photos of you frolicking in the surf, the resort flag waving in the breeze—among other things ..."

"You told them I'd never agree to do it."

"No, I didn't."

Pres stared. "Why the hell not?"

The greenish light from the dashboard threw shadows across Dom's craggy features. His thick, dark eyebrows moved closer together as he frowned. "Well, frankly, because I wasn't sure whether or not this might be something that would appeal to you."

"Posing *nude* for an international magazine . . . ? Mother of God, Dom!"

"I honestly didn't know. For chrissake, Pres, you skydive, you parasail, you bungee-jump, you windsurf, you mountain-climb, and when you really want to relax, you scuba-dive in shark-infested water. How was I to know whether or not having your picture snapped while in your birthday suit wouldn't provide some similar kind of thrill?"

"It doesn't."

"Okay, so now I know."

"I can't believe you thought I would. . . ." Pres shook his head.

"Well, *I* can't believe you would throw yourself out of an airplane at twelve thousand feet, with or without your clothes on," Dom told him.

"Tell the people from *Fantasy Man* thanks but no thanks. I don't want to be their most eligible anything."

"You can decline the photo spread, but the title's already yours, my friend."

Frustrated, Pres pushed his wet hair back from his face, then took another long drag on his cigarette. "I don't want it. I don't want this kind of publicity."

"You should have thought of that before you divorced Merrilee," Dom said. "According to the article in *Fantasy Man,* the fact that you not only walked away from Hollywood's brightest new starlet, but that you did it without paying a single penny in settlement or alimony placed you in the superhuman category."

Merrilee. God, she would have died for this kind of publicity. And she would have taken off her clothes for those pictures without batting an eye.... "Obviously they don't know the whole story," Pres told Dom.

"Obviously," he agreed. "The way I figure it, the only people who know the whole story are you and Merrilee."

"As it should be." Pres took the turn that led to

the private bungalows at the edge of the resort grounds.

"What do you want me to tell the news teams from *American Lifestyles* and *On-line Entertainment*? And the countless local news affiliates?"

"Tell them if they want to do a story about the resort, I'd be happy to accommodate them."

"*You're* the story here, pal. Not your resort. Although the free publicity for this place would be phenomenal if you talk to these guys. I don't see how you could turn it down."

Pres pulled alongside Dom's cottage. "I can turn it down because I don't feel like answering questions about my idea of a romantic evening, or my favorite place to have sex."

Dom laughed. "Yeah, well, you've got to use their lack of tact to your advantage. If they ask something like that, you bring it right back to a free commercial for the resort. You tell 'em your favorite place for creating the beast with two backs is in the king-size Jacuzzi tub that's a standard feature in every one of the resort's master suites. You see what I mean?"

"The beast with two backs? *That's* a nice one. Maybe I'll save that for the interview with the national news." Pres shook his head, stubbing out his cigarette in the overflowing ashtray. "Like it or not, I'm going to have to do these interviews, aren't I?"

Dom nodded. "The reporters are going to follow you around until you give in. Short of getting married tomorrow, I don't see what else you can do."

"That's a handy solution. Talk about out of the frying pan and into the fire."

"I was kidding."

"They're going to ask all kinds of questions about Merrilee, aren't they?" Pres asked.

"Probably."

"And it's not going to stop there, is it? After the interview airs, I'm going to be besieged by desperate single women."

Dom snorted. "We should all have such terrible problems."

"When you go to bed with a woman, do you have any trouble figuring out whether she's sleeping with you or the things your money can buy, including Hollywood contacts?" Pres asked sharply.

"Well, I don't have the kind of money that would make a difference, so..."

"Until you do, until you know what that's like, don't make light of my problems, okay?"

Dom was silent. "I'm sorry," he finally said. "I shouldn't have—"

Pres rubbed his forehead. "No, *I'm* sorry. I didn't mean to sound so—"

"I stepped over the line, boss."

"Don't start with the 'boss' crap. Yeah, you work for me, but so what? We're friends. You should be able to say anything—I don't want that to change. I'm just...I'm not having a very good day. The new owner of the Kirk Estate isn't going to sell for the figure I offered, and now this *Fantasy Man* thing..." Pres swore under his breath. "I need a shower and a beer—not necessarily in that order."

Dom opened the door of the car but then turned to look back at Preston. "You know this friends thing works both ways, pal. You should be able to say anything to me, too, you know."

Pres had to look away from Dominic's perceptive gaze. "Yeah," he said. "I know."

I met this woman today. Molly Cassidy. I

haven't been able to stop thinking about her. She doesn't seem to give a damn about money and she has the bluest eyes I've ever seen....

But he couldn't say it. He couldn't give even that much of himself away. He just shrugged.

"I'll have your secretary set up the interviews for tomorrow," Dom told him.

Pres nodded. "Thanks."

The morning sun was hot and the air was already humid. After the previous night's rain, it should have been clear and much cooler. At least it *would* have been if they were still living in the New York suburbs.

"Toto, we're not in Katonah anymore," Molly murmured.

Zander looked up. "You talking to me or yourself?"

"Myself," she said cheerfully, giving him a big smile as he helped her carry the laundry basket inside the Laundromat.

"Can I go next door to the pizza place? I saw some video games through the window."

Molly nodded. "Sure. Just help me get the

wash started, and I'll go over with you to scope it out, okay?"

"Okay."

"What did you think of your new school?" Molly asked as they sorted the laundry into two loads.

Zander looked up at her. "What?"

She repeated the question while he watched her lips and she signed the word *school*. His blue eyes were huge behind his glasses, and he gazed at her very seriously for several moments before answering. "It was pretty small," he finally said.

Molly nodded. "This town is a whole lot smaller than Katonah. There's gonna be only about twelve kids in your class—and that's both the fifth and sixth grades combined."

"So I'll be in a class with *sixth* graders?"

Molly nodded. "Yup. That's what your teacher, Mr. Towne, said. Weren't you paying attention when he was talking to us?"

Zander shrugged, digging through his mother's purse for her container of quarters. "He was kind of hard to understand."

Molly felt her heart sink. Zander's new teacher wasn't the warmest person in the world. In fact, she'd come away from this morning's meeting with the feeling that the man was less than pleased about the addition of Zander to his classroom. In fact, the first thing he'd said after the school principal had introduced them was that he had no intention of learning sign language.

No one expected him to learn sign language, and his statement came off sounding defensive and hostile.

"He had a funny voice," Zander continued.

Mr. Towne had had a rather thick Southern drawl. And he had a large, droopy mustache that had no doubt prevented Zander from being able to read the man's lips accurately.

And Zander would be in his classroom for not just the remainder of this year, but for all of next year as well.

"Hey, Zander. Molly. How's it going?"

The faintly raspy voice was unmistakable, and it made Molly's pulse leap. It was none other than Preston Seaholm, King of the Island, and newly crowned Most Eligible Bachelor of the Year. She'd seen him on the TV news the night before—wearing the same ratty clothing he'd had on when he'd helped her with her roof. He was still soaked, and he hadn't looked very happy that the news teams had caught him that way.

On camera, Pres had looked nothing like the billionaire playboy that he was. He'd looked more like a romantic, handsome castaway, forced to live by using only his wits and his physical strength. And with his wet T-shirt clinging to the hard muscles of his chest and arms, it wasn't hard to imagine him succeeding.

Fantasy Man, indeed.

Molly finished pouring the detergent powder into the washing machine, using the opportunity to take a deep breath and steady herself before she turned to face him.

He was smiling, and despite the glare of both the fluorescent lights and the afternoon sun pouring through the plate-glass windows, he managed to look as good as he had the night before.

Better.

He casually leaned against one of the washing machines. "These are my going-out-in-public clothes," he said. "What do you think?"

He'd shaved at some point between then and now. And instead of his ratty T-shirt and worn-out shorts and sneakers, he wore a dark pink polo

shirt that hugged his trim upper body and empha-
sized the powerful-looking muscles in his arms.
He also had on a crisp-looking pair of brown
Bermuda shorts. On his feet he wore simple
leather sandals and on his left wrist was an
expensive-looking gold watch. His eyes were still
hazel, though, and still quite warm.

"You look . . . well behaved without being too
stuffy," she told him, turning back to her laundry,
suddenly aware she'd been letting herself stare.
"The shorts and the polo shirt are traditional, but
a pink shirt . . . It gives you an air of individuality.
And the watch is a nice touch, of course—there to
remind the masses who you really are."

He laughed. "The masses?"

"Zander and me, for instance." Molly glanced
around the nearly empty room, taking in the rows
of humming washing machines and the clothes
being tossed about, visible through the glass port-
holelike windows in the fronts of the dryers.
"Please tell me you're not here to do your laundry.
There must be some law that prohibits persons in
a certain tax bracket from washing their own
clothes."

"Actually, I saw you come in, so I followed you."

"No," Molly said sternly.

Pres blinked, his Robert Redford smile slipping slightly. "Excuse me...?"

FOUR

"No," Molly said again. "I figured we could get this out of the way so that you're not wondering and I'm not waiting."

Preston looked confused for only the briefest moment, then he smiled again, amusement making his hazel eyes sparkle. "You think I followed you in here to make another offer on the estate?"

"Didn't you?"

"No. No, I was going to wait till later this afternoon to do that."

She closed both lids of the washing machines

and gathered up her purse. "Well, I'll save you the return trip. My answer's going to be no."

He lowered his voice. "You don't even know what it is that I intend to offer."

His soft, textured voice conjured up images of a different kind of offer altogether, images of candlelight and satin sheets and . . . Molly forced that rather breathtaking picture from her mind and turned to smile at Zander, who was watching the exchange with wide eyes. She then smiled in the general direction of Pres, without managing to meet his gaze. "Well, we were about to save the world from alien invasion and maybe get a slice of pizza to celebrate, weren't we, Z? We got a welcome basket from the Sunrise Key Chamber of Commerce that included a coupon for a sample slice and a free soda from Paulo's Pizzeria."

"Mind if I join you?"

Yes. Surprised by his question, and startled at the strength of her response to it, Molly found herself staring up into Preston Seaholm's eyes. She knew he could read her mind—he saw that *yes* written clearly across her face. There was a glint in his eyes and an edge to his smile that dared her to say it aloud.

But that would be flatly rude. Instead, she settled for slightly rude. "Why?"

"Because I'm hungry?" He said it as if it were a question, as if he wanted her to know that he wasn't being quite truthful either.

Zander tugged at her arm. "Can I go?"

Molly nodded and he was out the door in a flash. She followed her son at a slower pace, turning back to look at Pres. "It's not quite your style, is it? I mean, Paulo's Pizzeria hardly serves four-star cuisine."

"No, but it serves four-star *pizza*. And I oughta know—I own the place. Look, would it help when we talk if I took off my Rolex watch first? Yes, I have lots of money, but that doesn't mean I don't like pizza."

Outside the Laundromat, the heat and humidity were oppressive. But Molly stopped on the sidewalk to look up at Pres. "If you want me to forget that you're richer than God, you don't have to take off your watch or your clothes or . . . or . . . shave your head or . . . anything. You just have to stop trying to buy my house out from underneath me."

"It's my house. You just happen to be living there temporarily."

Molly laughed in disbelief. "Now, *that* was pompous."

"You were being honest," he protested. "I thought I would be too."

"That wasn't honesty. That was arrogance."

"I thought you said it was pomposity."

"It was both."

"I'm sorry. I didn't mean for it to be." He reached out and pulled a strand of hair free from where it had caught on her eyelashes.

Molly froze, startled both by the gentle sensation of his fingers barely touching her face and his quiet apology. For several breathtaking seconds she thought he might lean forward and kiss her. For several breathtaking seconds she found herself hoping that he would.

She turned away quickly, afraid her thoughts were mirrored in her eyes. Dear Lord, what was wrong with her? She'd gone the Prince Charming route once already, with Chuck, and *he'd* quickly turned into a frog.

She'd been alone for three years. Longer than that, really. The physical intimacies she'd shared with Chuck had been infrequent and less than perfect. But she'd learned to live without sex without a great deal of difficulty. She'd always figured her strongest passions were the intellectual kind.

So why, now, was she experiencing this overwhelming rush of physical attraction every time this man looked into her eyes?

Molly could feel heat rising in her face, and she ran for the door to the pizza parlor, throwing it open and stepping into the icy air-conditioned room.

Zander was already thoroughly engaged with one of the video games in the corner. He didn't hear her come in, of course, his attention glued to the advancing alien horde.

The room was empty, other than Z and the apron-clad man behind the counter. The man smiled at Molly. "Hot enough for you out there, huh?" But then his gaze shifted, and she knew that Pres had come in behind her. The pizza man's smile broadened. "Hey! How's it hanging, Pres? You know, I wanted to thank you again for inviting us to your party last week. Betty and I had the *best* time."

"Hey, Paulo." Pres had his Robert Redford smile on again, his eyes crinkling with either genuine or extremely well-acted pleasure. "Yeah, that was fun. I'm glad you had a good time. Can you get a couple slices for me and my friends, please?"

"Sure thing." Whistling, Paulo went to work.

"You're a benevolent ruler, aren't you?" Molly said quietly. "Everyone in town had something good to say about you."

Pres lifted his eyebrows. "Were you asking questions, trying to dig up some dirt on me? I'm honored you're that interested."

Molly slid onto the cool vinyl seat of the booth in front of the window, setting her oversized purse down next to her and the coupon for the free pizza next to the napkin holder. "My questions had nothing to do with you." She rested her chin in her hand as she gazed up at him. "I've been asking people for their recommendations—I'm trying to find someone to replace the roof of my house. *My* house. Everyone I asked suggested that I talk to you. Apparently you've always got some project or another under construction, and therefore you must know the local contractors better than anyone else on the island."

His eyes were lit with amusement and something else—something hotter and more dangerous. She looked away, but she could feel him watching her, studying her, his gaze as palpable as a touch.

Molly's hair was back in the casual ponytail that Pres guessed was her "default" hairstyle. A light fringe of bangs framed her pretty face. She wore only the slightest bit of makeup, and she looked impossibly fresh and young. The bright-colored picture of Mighty Mouse on her oversized T-shirt added to the youthful effect, as did her fraying cutoffs and bright pink flip-flop sandals.

"Actually, that has something to do with why I came looking for you," he told her. "I wanted to make sure you knew that the Kirk Estate is registered as one of Sunrise Key's historical buildings."

It wasn't, but as of five o'clock this afternoon, the newly formed Sunrise Key Historical Society would be firmly set in place, its rules and regulations approved by an emergency meeting of the town council.

"There are town codes that regulate alterations to historic buildings," he continued, sitting down across from her at the table. "The fact is, the Kirk Estate can be restored, but not renovated."

She gazed at him, her expression carefully guarded. "I don't see how that's going to be a problem," she said, "since restoration is more of what I had in mind."

"Restoration can be costly."

Molly didn't blink. "Of course."

"I don't know how much you've budgeted to make the necessary repairs." Pres didn't beat around the bush.

"My priority is the roof. I've budgeted nothing beyond that."

"The restoration regulations are restrictive," he told her. "I've worked on restorations before—and it's a real headache. It would be much easier for you to sell."

She smiled at that, genuine amusement dancing in her eyes. "I'm deeply touched by your concern."

Pres had to smile too. "You're really not going to sell to me, are you?"

She shook her head. "No, I'm not."

Otherwise Engaged

"What if I offered you a million dollars?"

Her smile wavered only slightly. "You'd never do that—the house isn't worth it."

She was right. As it was, the Kirk Estate wasn't worth even half that much. And he had no intention of buying at that kind of inflated price. He wanted the place, but not that badly.

"So are you going to give me a recommendation for the roof?" she asked.

"I recommend you sell me the house and—"

"Come on, Zander, time to go!" Molly started to slide out of the booth, but Pres caught her arm, holding her back.

"Don't," he said. "I was just making a joke. A *bad* joke, obviously."

His fingers were warm and broad and roughly callused, as if he did a great deal of outdoor work. Molly gazed down at his tan hand firmly clasped around the paler skin of her arm. His touch was electric and electrifying. She looked up to find him watching her, his eyes more green than brown, and charged with more of that very same electricity.

"Maybe we should forget about the house," he

- 57 -

said quietly, "and talk about having dinner tonight instead."

He was asking her out. Preston Seaholm, the island's resident Prince Charming, was asking her out.

Molly couldn't move. She couldn't answer him, couldn't pull her hand away, couldn't do more than gaze into his eyes. He reached up and touched the side of her face with his other hand, stroking the softness of her cheek with his thumb. This was trouble. This was a gigantic mistake. She knew that. But still she couldn't move.

"It occurs to me that pissing you off with my constant offers on the house may not be to my best advantage," he continued, still in that soft voice. "You don't want to sell? Okay. I can respect that. I can accept that. The hell with the house. Forget about it. Let's have dinner tonight."

As Pres watched, Molly nervously moistened her lips. She, too, was affected by the powerful connection, the odd sensation of awareness that seemed to flow between them. It was amazing. Sitting here like this, touching her like this, he could almost believe his own words. Forget about the house. It *was* forgotten. But only temporarily.

He *would* make damn sure that he stopped mentioning it in every other sentence, though. She *was* going to sell to him eventually, and at *his* price, but he'd keep that knowledge to himself for now.

"Here you go. Nice and hot."

Pres looked up to see Paulo balancing three paper plates filled with pizza slices. Molly sat back, slipping free from his grasp, a tinge of delicate pink on her cheekbones.

She was going to turn his dinner invitation down. Pres knew that as surely as he knew his own name. Damn. It frustrated him more than it should have, and that in turn frustrated him even further.

"Can I get you something to drink with that?" Paulo asked as he slid the plates onto the table.

"Something without caffeine for me and Zander, please," Molly said.

"And I'll have something loaded with caffeine," Pres countered. Paulo returned almost instantly with sodas, and Pres waited until he was gone before he turned back to Molly. "Why won't you have dinner with me?"

She glanced up at him. "How do you know I'm going to say no?"

"Aren't you?"

"Well, yeah..."

"So how come?"

She looked up at him again, and Pres knew whatever she was going to tell him, it wasn't going to be the real reason she didn't want to have dinner with him. She was usually blunt and direct, but he somehow knew that she wasn't going to be this time.

"Well, for one thing, you smoke."

Pres had to smile. "I think I can probably refrain from having a cigarette for a couple of hours."

"Yeah, but you smell like smoke all the time. It's..." She paused tactfully.

"What?"

"It's gross." Zander slid into the booth next to his mother. His bangs were standing straight up and his glasses were crooked. He took a bite of a pizza slice and smiled happily at Molly and Pres. "I kicked some alien butt."

"Congratulations and don't be rude." Molly picked up her own slice of pizza and took a bite. "Neither *gross* nor *butt* falls into the category of polite words." She glanced quickly at Pres, and he could see both amusement and chagrin in her eyes.

Gross. Zander thought he smelled gross. And Molly hadn't exactly disagreed.

"I know you're the most eligible bachelor in the universe, or whatever," Molly told him, "so we probably have no right in offering you personal grooming tips, but frankly, getting within a few feet of you is like cozying up to an ashtray. For a nonsmoker, that's a major turnoff."

"Smoking causes cancer," Zander interjected. "As well as making you stink." He worked hard to pronounce the *st* sound, but still it came out with a heavy lisp.

Preston sat back on the bench. "Well hey, guys, don't be shy," he said ruefully. "Don't hold back. Just come right out and tell me exactly what you think."

"Okay," Zander said, too young to recognize Pres's ironic tone. "Not only do you smell bad, but your stinky smoke is bad for other people too. *And* it's ruining the ozone layer."

"Thank you, Alexander," Molly said. "I think Mr. Seaholm gets the point." She was working hard to hold back both laughter and a smile.

Pres took the pack of cigarettes from his shirt pocket and studied them carefully. "Maybe I should quit." He glanced across the table at Molly. "If I quit, you'll have dinner with me, right?"

"I never said that."

"It was implied."

"No, it most certainly was not.... What am I worried about? You'll never quit."

"Wanna bet? I quit. There. See, I did it." He put the cigarette pack back in his pocket.

Molly snorted. "I can announce that I'm going to stand up and fly out the window, but that doesn't mean I'm actually going to be able to do it."

"I think it's great that you quit," Zander interjected.

"Thank you, Zander," Pres said. "At least *someone*'s on my side."

"If you were seriously going to quit," Molly pointed out, "you would have thrown the cigarettes out—not put them back in your pocket."

"I *will* throw them out. Later."

"After you have one last one?"

She'd hit the truth dead on. Pres couldn't deny

it, and she smiled. But her smile was more sad than triumphant.

Pres took the pack from his pocket and handed them to Zander. "Do me a favor and toss these in the trash can over near the door."

Molly gazed at Preston Seaholm. He might've had her son believing him, but she was no ten-year-old innocent. Even throwing the cigarettes away meant nothing. She knew quite well that he probably had another pack in his car, or in his desk at his office, or at home in his kitchen drawer.... And if not, he could simply buy another pack of cigarettes in just about every store on the island.

But Zander was sold.

"Hey, here's a story you're going to like," Pres said to Zander as he came back to the table. "I got a call this morning from a guy I know who lives on a boat out near St. John in the Virgin Islands. He owns a scuba-diving salvage company—if you lose something on the bottom of the ocean, he's the guy you call to go in after it and bring it back up for you."

Zander glanced at Molly, puzzlement in his eyes. She knew exactly which word had tripped him up. "Scuba," she told him in sign language, spelling out the letters of the word with her hands, saying it aloud as he watched her lips. She wasn't sure he understood, but he looked back at Pres expectantly.

"Scuba diving is when you put on a wet suit and you strap a big tank of air onto your back and swim underneath the water," Pres explained to the boy. "You don't have to come up to take a breath for a really long time because you're carrying all the air you'll need with you. You wear a mask on your face so you can open your eyes underwater, and flippers on your feet to help you swim faster. It's fun. It's the next best thing to being a fish."

Zander signed to Molly, "You wear what on your feet?"

"Flippers," she signed back. "Rubber flippers, kind of like ducks' feet."

He brightened, quickly moving his hands to say, "Like those people we saw on the beach?"

Molly glanced up at Pres, aware of him watching them, aware that he couldn't understand their silent communications. "Yesterday Zander and I saw some teenagers on the beach," she told him.

"They were wearing flippers and face masks, but I don't think they were scuba divers."

"Probably snorkelers," Pres said. "Snorkeling masks have a short tube that leads up to the air. There's no heavy tank to worry about. But you have to swim right up near the surface of the water. I like scuba diving better, myself."

"You know how to scuba-dive?"

Molly glanced at her son, aware that he was getting a serious case of hero worship.

"Yeah." Pres smiled at the boy. "And remember that guy I was telling you about? The one who lives on a boat? Well, he gave me a call this morning, because they had a big storm a couple of nights ago, too, and that storm kicked up the sand underneath the water and unburied a shipwreck."

Zander leaned forward. "A *what*?"

"Shipwreck," Pres repeated. "A ship—big sailing boat—that sank in the ocean during a storm, a long time ago. My friend thinks this one went down maybe as much as three hundred years ago."

Zander's eyes lit up. "You mean, like a pirate's ship?"

"It might've been."

"Carrying buried treasure?"

"I sure hope so." Pres's eyes were lit with that same excitement. "This friend of mine called to ask me if I wanted to help with the salvage effort."

"The *what*?"

Molly leaned forward, ready to explain the word to her son, sure Pres would be tired of the boy's constant questions. But as she spelled the new word out for Zander, Pres watched her hands.

"Salvage means to save all of the things on the ship that haven't been destroyed by being underwater for hundreds of years," Pres explained. "It means to pull all of the plates and spoons and pewter mugs that you find back up to the surface."

"Spoons?" Zander was scornful. "I'd rather find gold coins—you know, *real* treasure."

"But sometimes the spoons *are* the treasure," Pres told him. "Can you imagine owning a spoon that some sailor—or pirate—used back when Shakespeare was still alive?"

Zander didn't look convinced.

"Shakespeare," Pres repeated. "Another one of those *S* words." He mimicked one of the hand motions Molly had made, making a fist with his thumb on top of his fingers. "Is this an *S*?" he asked.

She nodded, startled that he would've been able to pick that up just from watching.

"*S* is one of the sounds you have trouble hearing, huh?" Pres asked, making the motion again with his hand.

Molly started to answer, but stopped. He'd asked Zander, not her. So many people, even those with the best intentions, talked over Z's head when asking questions about his hearing impairment. Even his new school principal, as nice as she was, had done that. But not Pres.

Zander nodded. "Yeah."

"And *sh* is hard for you to hear, too, right?" Pres asked. "How do you make an *H*?"

Zander showed him, and Pres imitated the position with his own hand.

"This is very cool," Pres told Zander. "You know, when you scuba-dive, when you're underwater, *nobody* can hear. Knowing sign language would be a real plus. Divers who knew sign language would have a real advantage."

"Are you going to dive down to that ship and look for the buried treasure?" Zander asked eagerly.

"I hope so," Preston said. "I'm going to fly down to St. John in a couple days."

"Isn't diving dangerous?" Molly couldn't keep the question from slipping out.

Pres glanced at her. "It has its moments of excitement," he said, as if that were a good thing. "Diving around a wreck can be particularly... challenging."

Zander could barely sit still. "Will you teach me to scuba-dive?"

Pres glanced up again, directly into Molly's eyes. No. He could read the crystal-blue warning quite clearly. "It's really not dangerous," he told her.

She turned to her son. "Mr. Seaholm couldn't possibly have the time to teach you." She turned back to Pres. "Isn't that right?"

Pres hesitated. It wasn't true. He did have time. And he liked Zander—almost as much as he liked Zander's mother. But she very obviously didn't want him teaching her son to scuba-dive. "You're only ten, right?"

Zander nodded. "Ten and a half."

"Well, you have to be twelve before you can take diving lessons and get certified. And if you're not certified, you can't dive."

Zander's face fell.

"But you need to know how to snorkel before you learn to dive, and I *can* teach you that."

"I guess so." Zander wasn't convinced.

Neither was Molly. "I don't know about snorkeling either. We'll have to talk about it."

"Can I have another quarter for the video game?" Zander asked.

Molly fished in her purse, but Pres beat her to it, pulling a quarter from his pocket and handing it to her son. In a flash the boy was gone. Molly dug a quarter free and put it down on the table in front of Pres.

"You're kidding, right?" he asked, pushing it back in front of her.

"No." She pushed it back to his side of the table.

Pres put his hand over hers, trapping both it and the quarter on the table.

"First of all," he said, "learning to scuba-dive is *not* dangerous. Beginners' lessons are taught in a swimming pool. And secondly, if you're not going to let me teach him to snorkel, you can at least let me treat your kid to a lousy video game."

She looked up at him, and he was taken aback by the vulnerability in her eyes. "The thought of him learning to scuba-dive scares me to death, and I know if he learns to snorkel he'll want to learn to dive."

"Then maybe you should learn too. I could give you both lessons. And then you'd see it's not so—"

"I don't think so."

"Maybe you should try it. Sometimes all you need is just to try something once, and then it's not so frightening." He was talking about more than scuba diving now. He was talking about her reluctance to go out with him, to have dinner, to acknowledge the hot attraction that flared between them.

"I'm not a strong swimmer either," Molly told him.

"So we can take it slow."

Molly smiled at him suddenly, a sweet, rueful smile. "Why are we suddenly talking in code?"

"Because it's easier that way. For some reason, you're determined to keep your distance from me. And if I were to just come right out and tell you that I can't stop thinking about you..."

Molly covered her sudden rush of confusion with a laugh, pulling her hand out from underneath his. "I thought it was my *house* you couldn't stop thinking about."

"What house?" Preston said.

"You're wasting your time," she told him. "Both on me *and* my house."

Pres just smiled, glancing at his watch. "I have to get going." He stood up. "I'll call you tomorrow with a recommendation for a roofer, okay?" He started for the door, raising his voice so Zander could hear him. "Catch you later, Zander!"

Then he was out the door. Molly found herself staring after him, watching his surefooted, confident stride as he walked away. She pulled her gaze away, suddenly uncomfortably aware that she was staring at the man's perfect rear end.

Zander looked up from the alien horde long

enough to glance back at his mother. "Pres is *so* cool."

Cool? Not quite the word Molly had been thinking. Pres Seaholm was hot. *Too* hot. And she wasn't the type who ever played with fire.

It was almost a shame.

FIVE

"MR. SEAHOLM, how much exactly are you worth?"

"Mr. Seaholm, can you tell us your ex-wife's reaction to your being chosen Most Eligible Bachelor of the Year?"

"Mr. Seaholm, why won't you pose for the photo spread in *Fantasy Man* magazine?"

"Mr. Seaholm—"

Pres could see Dom standing at the edge of the resort's main covered deck, back behind the rows of seated reporters and news cameras. Dom held his gaze, silently offering support as Pres approached the wall of microphones that had been set up in front of a wooden podium.

"I think," he began, and paused, waiting for the hubbub to die down. "I think this would work out a whole lot better if I took questions one at a time." He motioned to a friendly-looking gray-haired lady seated in the front row. He'd let himself warm up with a few easy, polite questions, and work his way up to the big-haired blonde in the leopard-print dress who was sure to ask him about his ex-wife. "Ma'am?"

"Camilla Carter, *Southwestern Florida News,*" the sweet-faced older lady identified herself. "Mr. Seaholm, is it true that during her so-called marriage to you, Merrilee Fender was also sleeping with studio head Robert Taggart, as well as director Richie Guiness?"

Oh, God. So much for starting with the easy questions. The deck was nearly silent as Pres looked back at Dom again. The dark-haired man was slowly shaking his head in disgust.

Pres leaned toward the bank of microphones. "I'm sorry, Ms. Carter," he said. "Miss Fender seems to have failed to show up for this press conference. You'll have to save your questions for her for the next time you see her."

A man stood up in the third row, blinking owlishly at him from behind a thick pair of glasses. "Mr. Seaholm, will you comment on the rumors that the dozens of cocktail waitresses and maids you have working at the Seaholm Resort are in truth your own private harem?"

What? Pres had to laugh. "You're kidding, right?"

The owl man didn't crack a smile. "No, sir."

"Where the hell do you guys *get* these questions?"

"Is that a denial, sir?"

"Damn right it's a denial!"

Another man stood up. "Mr. Seaholm, your divorce agreement with Merrilee Fender included no alimony payments or financial settlement of any kind, the implication being that Miss Fender was desperate enough to be released from the marriage to forgo any financial reimbursement. The initial expectation was that there was another man involved, but it's been two years and Miss Fender is still unattached. Current speculation concerns your ability—or inability, as it were—to perform sexually. Would you care to comment?"

Current speculation . . . His inability to perform sexually . . . Dear Lord, were there really people sitting around out there spending their time wondering if he and Merrilee had divorced because he was unable to get it up? Pres looked across the deck at Dominic, who had covered his eyes with one hand. Dom couldn't help him. No one could help him here.

He wanted to turn and walk away. He almost did, but he was aware of the cameras on him, watching, waiting. If he walked away, it would look as if he were confirming everything the reporter had said. He knew he shouldn't give a damn what other people thought, but in this particular case, he did.

So he didn't simply leave. Instead, he fixed the reporter with his iciest stare.

"What gives you the right," he said softly, dangerously, "to come here and ask me questions about my sexual ability?" He included the rest of the reporters as he swept his gaze around the room and his voice grew louder. "What gives *any* of you the right to ask me questions that are so personal, they'd make your mothers blush? For the record, ladies and gentlemen, my sexual relationship with my ex-wife was *not* where my marriage failed. Also for the record, I didn't ask to be named Most Eligible *Anything*. I didn't want the title, still don't want the title, but I was told it was too late, *Fantasy Man* magazine had already awarded me the extremely dubious honor."

Pres paused, and a reporter stood up.

"Mr. Seaholm, is there truth to the rumors that you are a violent man?"

Pres knew in that instant that there was nothing he could say, no amount of guilt or fist-shaking, no pleas for respect and decency that would make these insane questions end. He looked across the deck again, and met the sympathy in Dom's gaze. Short of getting married, Dom had told him, there was nothing he could do to avoid this torture.

Short of getting married...

With a flash of inspiration, Pres knew exactly how to end this ridiculous game once and for all.

"I didn't want to have to do this," he said into the bank of microphones. "I value my privacy above just about everything, and consider my personal relationships to be very private matters. But the truth is," he lied, "since several days ago I'm no longer an 'eligible bachelor.' The truth is, I'm engaged to be married."

Married. Pres Seaholm was engaged to be *married*. Molly didn't know which she should feel more disgusted about—the fact that the man had asked her out to dinner despite being attached, or the fact that the man's marital status was considered worthy of the eleven o'clock news.

She flipped the channel on the remote control to another station. A dark-haired man was speaking. There was a caption identifying him as Dominic Defeo, Seaholm Resort.

"I'm sorry, Mr. Seaholm has no intention of disclosing his fiancée's name," he said in a disdainful drawl that dripped old New England money.

"Mr. Seaholm may have no intention of revealing the identity of his mysterious fiancée," the news anchor said, smiling into the camera, "but this photo, taken by a reporter from the *Florida Sun Times* just may have given his secret away."

Molly dropped the remote.

That was *her* picture on the screen. With Preston Seaholm. They were sitting across from one another in the window booth at Paulo's Pizzeria. The photo was taken at some distance, through the windowpane, but it was definitely the two of them. He was holding her hand. When had she let him hold her hand . . . ? The quarter. She was trying to give him back his damned quarter. He was leaning forward, his gaze intense, almost hungry. And she—she was smiling at him. Lord, look at the way she was grinning foolishly at him, looking for all the world as if she were welcoming his attention.

"Local sources identify the young woman as Molly Cassidy, a new resident of Sunrise Key."

There was a rapping on the French doors that led to the back patio, and Molly jumped.

Preston Seaholm was standing outside in the dim moonlight. He glanced from her to the television set as she scrambled to her feet, turning off the TV as she passed it, and unlocked the door.

"I'm sorry," he said as she let him in. "I didn't mean to scare you. It just . . . I didn't want to stand out front where everyone could see me, and...I guess you've seen the news."

Molly crossed her arms. Cool and collected Pres Seaholm was flustered and embarrassed. It would have been amusing if the entire situation hadn't been so obviously upsetting to him. She'd watched the interview, seen his angry reaction to the insensitive questions he'd been asked.

"They think I'm your fiancée," she said, locking the door behind him.

"I'm sorry," he said again. "I had no idea they would jump to conclusions that way."

"Your real fiancée must not be too happy about all this."

He wasn't wearing his so-called going-out-in-public clothes. He was dressed in a softly faded black T-shirt and a colorful pair of shorts. "I don't really have a fiancée," he admitted, chagrin in his eyes.

He didn't have a fiancée. So what? Big deal. That news shouldn't make her feel so damned happy. It shouldn't make her feel anything at all.

"I made it up to get out of that Most Eligible Bachelor of the Year thing," he continued. "I didn't realize reporters were following me around, taking pictures of us like that. I had no intention of dragging anyone else into this. Particularly not you."

"Well, I'm here," Molly said. "I'm all over the evening news—at least all over Channel Ten."

"I've already issued a statement to the press explaining that we have a business relationship. Nothing more."

Suddenly aware of the exposure from the windows and the blackness of the night outside, Molly began closing the blinds. "And you, of course, hold hands with all of your business acquaintances."

He wasn't amused. "I feel really awful about this, Molly."

She glanced back at him. "Relax—we'll get through it."

"I'm not sure I'd be so understanding if you were the one who yanked me into the public eye."

"Maybe the publicity will spark some interest in Chuck's books," Molly said lightly. "I could use an extra couple hundred bucks in royalty payments next year."

Pres was staring at her as if she were from

another planet. But then he laughed, shaking his head. "Somehow I expected you'd be angry about this. I'm . . . amazed you're not."

"What's the worst that can happen?" Molly asked. "I get asked a few questions." She shrugged. "It's only a matter of time before the reporters find out how deadly boring I am."

Pres couldn't believe what she'd just said. Boring? Was she crazy? She was so much the opposite of boring. He was standing in her living room, his pulse rate elevated just from being in her presence.

He followed her as she moved to shut the last of the blinds. "You're kidding, right?"

Her hair was down loose around her shoulders and shiny clean. Her nose and cheeks were a healthy shade of pink. She wasn't a beauty queen—not the way Merrilee had been. But there was something about Molly, a sensitivity, an awareness in her blue eyes, an aura of razor-sharp intelligence softened by a serious helping of kindness and sincerity. Whatever it was, it was something that Merrilee never had, something Merrilee would never have.

And it was something that made Molly attractive in a way that Merrilee would never be.

Molly backed away and bumped into the window. She was trapped, and Pres was still moving toward her. She cleared her throat nervously as he took her hand.

"You smell like cigarettes."

That stopped him. She watched his eyes, saw him consider hiding the truth for only about one tenth of a second before he spoke. "Yeah," he admitted. "I didn't know that the second I quit all hell was going to break loose. I've been smoking all night."

"It's not so easy, is it?" She broke free, slipping past him and escaping into the middle of the room.

"I didn't think it was going to be easy." He smiled ruefully. "I just didn't think it was going to be this hard."

"Some of those questions the reporters asked you..." Molly stood behind the rocking chair, using it as a sort of a shield. "It was awful."

Pres winced. "How much of the interview did they play?"

"Let's just say that the entire Florida viewing

public knows that impotence is *not* on your list of problems."

"Of course they'd play *that* part." He ran his hands through his hair, clearly embarrassed. "Mother of God." He turned back to her. "And you're not afraid of the questions they're going to ask *you*?"

"Like I told you—I'm boring. What can they possibly ask that I'd be unable to answer? No, I haven't slept with you. And no, I haven't slept with Merrilee Fender, either...." She shrugged. "You're just some guy who's trying to buy my house. The hand-holding bit and the dinner invitation were just attempts to charm me into selling you the property."

Pres was leaning back against the windowsill, watching her intently. "You don't really believe that, do you?"

She crossed her arms. "Please. I'm hardly your type."

"Four major networks and five newspaper syndicates had no trouble at all believing you're enough my type to be my fiancée," he told her.

"Yeah, well, they would believe Medusa was

your type if they thought it would sell more advertising."

He pushed himself forward, standing up and digging his wallet from the back pocket of his shorts. "Look, I want to try to make this up to you." He took a business card from his wallet and held it out to Molly. "Here."

She met him halfway across the big living room and took the card from him, careful their fingers didn't touch. "What's this?"

Emerson James, the card read, along with a local phone number.

"He's a roofer," Pres explained, "specializing in historical restorations. He owes me a favor—a *big* favor. He'll fix this roof for you at cost. I've already put in a call to his office. He'll be contacting you tomorrow."

At *cost.* Molly gazed at Pres. "I don't know what to say."

He shook his head. "You don't have to say anything. I feel as if I've somehow tainted you—God, I didn't mean to do that." He turned away. "I better go."

Molly stopped him with a hand on his arm. His

skin felt warm beneath her fingers, and she could feel the tension in the tightness of his muscles.

"Thank you," she said.

Pres looked down at her. "Helping you with the roof doesn't begin to make up for the grief I've caused you."

"It's not that big a deal. Everything's going to be all right," she told him.

As if on sudden impulse, he pulled her in close, holding her tightly against him. Molly didn't resist his embrace. She knew he needed to be held. And to her surprise, she found that she had a similar need.

His arms felt sinfully good wrapped around her, and she closed her eyes, resting her head against his chest. He was even more solid than she'd expected, all hard muscles and broad shoulders and powerful legs. He smelled like cologne and cigarette smoke, and for the first time in her life the smoky smell didn't bother her.

He sighed. "I have to stay away from you."

Molly kept her eyes tightly closed as she nodded. "That would probably be a good idea."

"It's a damned lousy idea."

His vehemence rumbled in his chest, and Molly lifted her head to look up at him.

Big mistake.

Their gazes caught and sparked and Molly knew he was going to kiss her. He lowered his head.

"Don't," she said. "Pres, don't."

He stopped, mere inches from her mouth, pulling back to a safer distance. "Ashtray," he said, chagrin in his eyes. "Right?"

Ashtray? She made the connection—she'd told him that getting close to him was like cozying up to an ashtray. In truth, that had nothing to do with her not wanting to kiss him. In truth, it was pure fear that stopped her. Fear of getting in too deep, fear of falling, once again, for a man she knew nothing about.

She nodded, letting him believe the easiest explanation. "Ashtray," she echoed weakly, and he pulled away.

"Sorry."

Pres stood with one hand on the doorknob. He knew he should go, and he knew he didn't want to. But what he wanted and what Molly needed were two entirely different things.

She looked up at him, her blue eyes so subdued.

Pres gazed at her, still amazed at how soft she'd felt and how perfectly she'd fit in his arms. "I'm sorry," he said again.

He opened the French doors and vanished into the night.

S I X

"Is THAT supposed to be a boat?"

Pres turned and looked at Zander, who had appeared behind him and was staring critically over his shoulder at his watercolor painting. "Yeah."

Zander nodded, his glasses crooked as usual. "It's good."

"No, it's not."

"Better than I could do."

"I wonder. I was just thinking that from certain angles it looks more like a hippopotamus."

"A what?"

Pres turned and faced the boy, letting him see

his lips. "A hippopotamus. You know, big animal, wide mouth. Lives in Africa . . . ?"

Zander nodded, turning back to study the painting. He couldn't hide his smile as he glanced at Pres out of the corner of his eyes. "It's the right color."

"I keep wanting to add ears and eyes right here," Pres said, pointing to his painting.

"Maybe you should."

"Who'd want a picture of a hippo swimming in the Gulf of Mexico?"

"I would. I could give it to Mom for her birthday."

"Your mom's birthday is coming up?"

"Yeah—in a couple weeks." Zander angled his head to look at the picture again. "I bet she'd like it. It would be . . . unique. That's my word for today. *Unique*. It means special."

"That's a pretty hard word." Pres sat back in his chair and fumbled in his pocket for his cigarettes. "And you learn one every day?"

The cigarettes weren't there. He'd quit the night before for good, after not kissing Molly. But God, it hadn't even been twelve hours yet, and he was dying for a smoke. His hands were shaking—

no wonder his damned boat looked like a hippo. This not smoking could very well kill him. But if it meant he'd get a chance to kiss Molly Cassidy, then dammit, he'd die smiling. He pulled out a pack of gum, offering it to Zander too.

The boy eagerly took a piece. "Thanks." They both unwrapped the gum and chewed in silence for a moment. "The daily word is Mom's idea," Zander finally told Pres after his gum was soft enough to talk around. "I learn how to say it right, and we both learn how to sign it." He held up the pointer finger of his left hand, and with his right thumb and index finger, he took hold of it and lifted both hands upward. "That's the sign for *unique.*"

Pres imitated the movement. "That's *cool.*"

Zander brought both hands up to his face, palms in, and flapped his fingers as if fanning himself. "No, *that's* cool," he said with a grin.

"Very funny. Hey, you know, I was serious about wanting to learn how to sign. Will you teach me?"

Zander made several rapid motions with his hands. He did them again slower. "If you teach me to swim, I'll teach you to sign," he interpreted.

The sign for *teach* looked as if Zander were pulling information out of his forehead.

"I don't know the sign for *scuba* or *snorkel*," he told Pres, "but that's what I really want to learn how to do. I know my mom doesn't want me to, though."

"Remember you have to be twelve before you can actually start training to get certified to dive. But maybe by then we can talk Molly into taking scuba-diving lessons too."

"*Mom?*" Zander gave Pres a disbelieving look.

"Speaking of your mom, does she know you're down here at the beach?"

Zander glanced over his shoulder, and Pres turned also to look back toward the Kirk Estate. From where he was sitting, he could just see the red-tiled roof over the tops of the trees.

"I told her I was going outside," Zander said. "If she wants me, she'll page me."

"You have a pager?"

"Yeah, we just got one. The house is so big, and I can't always hear Mom when she shouts for me. She says it was driving her crazy. This way, she pages me, and we meet in the kitchen. She says it's a lot more dignified. *Dignified* was yesterday's word."

"Your mom's pretty cool." Pres made the sign for *cool*.

Zander grinned. "Why don't you come up to the house? It's almost time for breakfast. Mom makes the best muffins. And I just got a whole bunch of new CDs from the library. We listen to something new every morning at breakfast. My two favorite composers are Wolfgang Mozart and Alan Menken. Mom says Menken is Mozart reincarnated. That was one of last week's words. I think Mozart's probably pretty happy to be called Alan this time around instead of Wolfgang. Who's your favorite composer?"

Pres shrugged. "I don't really have one."

"You *don't*?" Zander's eyes were huge with disbelief.

"I don't listen to music that much."

"You *should*. Everyone should. I love music more than anything in the world. I wish I could be an opera singer when I grow up."

"Maybe you can."

Zander quickly shook his head. "Nah. But you should *definitely* start listening to music. I can tell you which of the CDs in the library are the best, if you want."

Pres had to smile. "I didn't even know the library *had* CDs."

"The Sunrise Key Library doesn't have very many," Zander told him. "So are you going to come up and have breakfast?"

Pres shook his head. "I don't think that's such a good idea."

"Because of what it says in the newspaper—about you and Mom getting married, only none of that's true?"

"Yeah."

Zander sat down next to him, picking up a stick and drawing a line in the dry sand. "Were you really married to that movie star?"

"Yeah."

Zander thought about that for all of two seconds. "She's pretty," he said, "but I bet she can't play Donkey Kong Two the way Mom can."

Pres had to laugh. "No, I think you're right." He looked at the boy. "You know, your mom is pretty too."

Zander gave him a long look. "But she's not a movie star."

"Thank God."

Zander stood, brushing the sand off his hands. "I gotta go. My pager's going off. It's got a silent setting, and it just shakes. It's funny—you want to feel it?"

Pres took the pager that Zander offered him. It vibrated in his hand. "That definitely feels funny."

"You sure you don't want to have some breakfast? You could hear some good music and Mom wouldn't mind...."

Pres wasn't convinced about that. He shook his head, handing the pager back to the boy. "No thanks, Zander. Just tell Molly..." What? "Tell her I said hi."

Zander gave him another of those long, appraising looks. "I'll tell her you smell better today too."

Pres laughed. "Thanks."

Molly didn't like going to Millie's Market.

It didn't have anything to do with the owner, Millie Waters, who was as warm and friendly as she was large. It didn't have anything to do with the vast selection of fruits and vegetables—all of them incredibly fresh, some of them from Millie's own organic garden.

It had to do with that old, faded photograph of Chuck, hanging up near the cash register. He stood next to a younger, only slightly slimmer Millie, gazing unsmilingly and so seriously into the camera, as mysterious and full of secrets as he ever was. He seemed to watch Molly every time she so much as set foot in the store.

Chuck had always had so many secrets. But today Molly had one of her own—one she was trying to hide even from herself. One having to do with *Fantasy Man*'s Most Eligible Bachelor of the Year, no less. The sad truth was, she hadn't been able to stop thinking about Pres Seaholm all day.

It was all about sex. Had to be. After all, it had been three years since she'd been with a man. Longer, Molly thought, glancing up at the photo of Chuck.

She grabbed a shopping cart and headed toward the back of the market, where the fresh produce was displayed. She had to stop thinking about Pres Seaholm and remember to get another box of cornflakes. This morning, Zander had opened the box to discover it had been infested with fire ants and...

A flashbulb went off in her face.

"Molly Cassidy?"

"Excuse me, Miss Cassidy, will you comment on Preston Seaholm's statement that you are allegedly *not* his fiancée?"

"Miss Cassidy, we've had a tip that Mr. Seaholm was seen entering your house by the back door last night at eleven-fifteen P.M. Can you tell us what you and he did until he left at approximately quarter to midnight?"

"Miss Cassidy, what exactly *is* your relationship with Preston Seaholm?"

Another flashbulb went off, and Molly had to laugh. "You're taking pictures of me *grocery shopping*? Get a life, guys. Come on...."

"Enough!" Millie was bellowing. "That's enough! I won't have this in my store! I demand that you leave—not you, Molly. But everyone else—out. Get out!"

"Miss Cassidy, *On-line Entertainment* is willing to offer you fifty thousand dollars for an exclusive television interview, providing your perspective on Merrilee Fender and Preston

Seaholm's divorce," one of the reporters said to Molly in a low voice.

"But I don't even *know* Merrilee Fender," she started to say.

But just as quickly as the reporters had descended upon her, they turned.

Pres Seaholm had come into the store.

Millie was standing up on the checkout counter, shaking with anger and threatening to call Liam Halliday, Sunrise Key's sheriff.

The reporters began calling out Pres's name, adding to the noise and chaos, asking *him* their ridiculous questions, every one of which he ignored.

Molly could do nothing but stand and stare.

Pres was wearing a dark-colored business suit, complete with gleaming white shirt and power tie, and that, combined with his slicked-back hair and the tight expression on his face, made him look completely, thoroughly formidable. His eyes were all but shooting sparks as he searched the room, softening only slightly with relief as he found Molly and met her gaze.

He pushed his way none too gently through the crowd.

"Are you all right?" He ignored the reporters, speaking to her as if she were the only person in the room.

Molly nodded. "Yeah. I'm fine. It's just...it's silly." She shrugged, suddenly intensely aware both of the warmth of his hands on her bare arms and of how happy she was to see him. She smiled foolishly up at him. "I mean, if they really want to take pictures of me buying zucchini..."

Flashbulbs were going off again, and Pres pulled Molly with him toward the back of the store, trying to shield her from the cameras. Millie Waters had moved toward the back delivery door, and she closed and locked it behind them as soon as they went out.

And just like that, they were suddenly, blessedly alone.

"Are you sure you're okay?"

Molly nodded again.

It had to be nearly one hundred degrees out there in the little alley behind the market. Pres felt the dark fabric of his jacket absorbing the heat of the brilliant afternoon sun like some kind of black hole. But he didn't care. He didn't care about anything but this woman who was gazing up at him with such a mixed expression on her face.

She might not be willing to admit it, but a substantial part of her was as glad to see him as he'd been to see her. Pres knew that without a doubt. And he knew in that instant, if he pulled Molly into his arms and crushed his mouth to hers, she would kiss him with the same unrestrained passion.

But he couldn't forget that it would be only a matter of moments before the reporters found their way into this alley.

And he couldn't forget Molly's son.

"Where's Zander?" Pres asked, his voice sounding raspy in the stillness. He took her hand and tugged her along with him toward the end of the rank-smelling little alley.

"He's over at the Congregational church. The Sunday school's organizing a musical revue, and he volunteered to help. Why?"

"Come on, I've got a car waiting."

Molly stared. A car, indeed. It was a stretch limousine, black and sleek, complete with privacy glass. "It matches your suit," she said.

"I had a business lunch over on the mainland."

Pres opened the door for her and all but pushed her inside. The seats were covered in real leather. There was a TV and a VCR and a bar and even a computer. "When I left the meeting, my driver had picked up a newspaper for me. That's when I saw this."

Pres handed her the newspaper, open to the lifestyles section, as he climbed into the limo after her. "Drive, Lenny," he ordered the driver through an intercom before he even shut the door behind him. "To the Congregational church."

Molly stared at the picture in the newspaper. Zander was in that picture, wearing his favorite superhero T-shirt and his cutoff jeans. He was standing next to Pres, who was sitting in a beach chair, eyes covered by a pair of aviator sunglasses, hair blowing in the ocean breeze. They were both smiling at each other—laughing, really. It was a nice picture. A *really* nice picture.

Except it was on the front page of the B section of the *Florida Sun Times*.

Molly read the caption aloud. " 'Practicing for Father's Day? Sunrise Key resident and *Fantasy Man* magazine's currently reigning Most Eligible Bachelor of the Year, Preston Seaholm, relaxes on the beach this morning with Alexander'—Lord, where did they get his name?—'son of Molly Cassidy, whom the billionaire insists is *not* his mysterious bride-to-be. Sure, we believe you, Pres.'"

She looked up at Preston, his desire for haste suddenly making sense. "Oh, my God. You think the reporters might know that Zander's over at the church?" She leaned forward and pressed the intercom button. "Drive faster, Lenny."

"We're almost there," Pres said.

Molly turned, watching out the window. She could see an *On-line Entertainment* news van in the church parking lot.

"*Damn.*" Pres's jaw was tightly clenched. "Molly, I am *so* sorry about this. This morning when I was talking to Zander, I didn't stop to think—"

Molly reached over and took his hand. "Frankie Paresky's in charge of the kids while they're at the church. There's no way she would let a news team within twenty feet of Zander."

Lenny pulled the limo up alongside the main entrance to the church. Molly could see the reporters and camera teams climbing out of the air-conditioned comfort of their cars and vans.

She scrambled for the door, but Pres was there first. "Why don't you wait here?" he asked. "Let me go in and get him."

"No way."

"Molly, if they get footage of us together, they're going to assume—"

"What? That in a town of only six hundred and fifty-seven people we wouldn't have happened to have met? We're friends, big deal."

"You're in my limousine."

"So? We've both still got our clothes on, and unless you've got your clothes off, it doesn't count. Didn't you know that?"

Pres shook his head. "Molly—"

"If they can't believe we're just friends, that's their problem."

"It's *our* problem, and you know it. And it looks as if it's become Zander's problem now too."

Molly's face hardened as she looked out the window at the brick church. "How could they do this to a kid? Doesn't it occur to them that he might get scared, with questions being shouted at him and those big TV cameras? With all that noise, Zander wouldn't even be able to hear what anyone's saying. He's only ten years old, and he's hearing-impaired, dammit." She looked back at Pres, her eyes suddenly filled with tears. "I want my kid."

Pres knew with sudden extreme clarity exactly what he had to do. He'd gotten Molly and Zander into this, it was up to him to get them out. "I'm going out first to run interference with the reporters," he told Molly. "You go to the church's kitchen door. Bring Zander right back out and into the limo." He keyed the intercom button. "Lenny, as soon as Molly gets out, back around and pull as close as you can to the kitchen door. Then wait for my signal, okay?"

Molly nodded.

Pres smiled, a hot, fierce smile not unlike the one he'd given her up on the roof during the thunderstorm. "Let's do it."

In a flash, he was out of the limo, moving to intercept the news teams.

Molly followed him out into the sweltering humidity of the Florida afternoon and hurried toward the far church door.

"Mr. Seaholm! Mr. Seaholm!" Over her shoulder, Molly saw the crowd of reporters seem to swallow Pres up. She could see only the reddish-gold glint of his hair as it reflected the late-afternoon sun.

The kitchen door was locked, but she could hear the bolt being thrown back. The door creaked open and Frankie Paresky pulled her inside, into the church kitchen, quickly locking the bolt behind her.

"He's all right," Frankie told Molly, before she could even ask. "Zander was out on the playground with the other kids when the reporters first arrived. One of the older girls ran to get me, and I came screaming out of the kitchen. I think *I* scared Zander more than the reporters did!"

"Mommy!" Zander ran toward her, and she caught him in both arms, picking him up and holding him tightly. He didn't object to being held like a baby. He just hugged her.

"They were asking him questions they shouldn't've been asking a little boy." Frankie spoke in a low voice, her dark eyes blazing. She smiled suddenly. "I told them exactly where they should go and what they should do when they get there, and I'm afraid my language wasn't exactly biblical."

Zander lifted his head. "She said they should—"

Frankie slipped a hand over the boy's mouth. "Thanks, Zander, we won't repeat it."

He wiggled free from Molly's arms. "Mom, did you know Frankie is a private eye like Sherlock Holmes?"

"*Exactly* like Sherlock Holmes," Frankie added. "Except he's a guy, and I'm not. And he lives in England and I don't. And he lived a hundred years ago, and I live now. And he's a fictional character, and I'm not.... At least I *hope* I'm not...."

Zander laughed.

Molly hugged him, grateful that he was still able to smile, and knowing much of that was due to Frankie Paresky's upbeat, irreverent attitude. "Thank you so much."

Frankie nodded. "Zander's a good kid. It was my pleasure."

"We better get out of here. We'll see you on Sunday."

"Sure you don't want to wait until that scum leaves?"

"Pres's limo is right outside."

"His limo?" Frankie's eyebrows went up. "Preston Seaholm's limo. Well, well. Are you sure there's no truth to all these rumors about a wedding?"

Zander looked at her, and Molly made a face at him.

"I've had maybe six conversations with the man," she told Frankie. "That's hardly enough to base an entire lifetime relationship on."

"He's a nice guy," Frankie said. "Maybe a little flaky at times, but who isn't, right? You could do far worse than a billionaire, you know."

"See you on Sunday," Molly repeated as she unlocked the bolt and opened the door.

There was the limo, mere feet from the church. Molly quickly opened the door and pushed Zander in, climbing in after him.

Her son was in total awe. "Whoa. What is *this*?"

"Pres's limousine." She tried to say the words casually.

"This is *awesome*! Pres is *awesome*!"

"Please fasten your seat belts." A voice—it had to be Lenny's—came from a little speaker in the ceiling. "I'm waiting for Pres to give me some sort of signal. When he gives it, we're going to move fast, so hold on."

Waiting for Pres. Pres was on a first-name basis with his limo driver. Why didn't that surprise her? He was on a first-name basis with everyone else in town—including her ten-year-old son.

Molly fastened her own seat belt as Zander strapped himself in. Leaning forward, she could see the reporters and cameras. She saw Pres break free of the crowd and start running toward them.

"That looks like a signal to me," Lenny said, and he stepped on the gas.

Molly leaned toward the door, pushing it open just as the limo screeched to a stop. Pres threw himself inside, and they were off again.

Zander was all eyes, taking in Pres's designer suit and slicked-back hair.

Pres flipped on the intercom. "Take us back to the resort, Len."

Molly raised her voice. "Make that the Kirk Estate, Lenny. Zander and I want to go home."

"Take the scenic route," Pres countered, then

turned to face Molly, evenly meeting her gaze. "There's probably already a crowd of reporters waiting for you at home. I'd feel a lot better if you stayed in a suite at the resort—as my guest—until this dies down."

Molly's heart was in her throat. Stay at the resort... She could just picture the two of them being shown into some elegant hotel suite. "Oh, that's really going to make things die down—me and Zander staying in some fancy suite, living under your roof?"

He smiled at that. "It's a really large roof. Besides, I don't live in the main resort building. I have a bungalow on the edge of the property. Although I'd like it if you'd allow me to join you for dinner. We could order room service—it would be very private."

"Room service," Zander breathed.

Pres glanced at the boy and smiled. "Mostly private," he added, meeting Molly's eyes.

She knew what he was thinking. With Zander there, it wouldn't be as private as he'd like it to be. And there was no doubt in her mind that Pres wanted dinner to have one course more than what was on the menu.

"Mom." Zander tugged on her arm. "Room service! *Can* we? Please? It would be like a real vacation."

"I have around-the-clock security teams at the resort. It's private property. They'll make sure the reporters stay far away from you. And from Zander."

Molly wasn't convinced. "And how long would we have to hide there, under your security teams' protection? A week? Two? Longer?" She shook her head, turning to include Zander. "No. If we run and hide, everyone's going to assume that we have something that needs to be hidden."

But she did have something to hide. She had to keep hidden the fact that Pres's dinner invitation—and the unspoken invitation she could see in his eyes—had sparked a fire deep within her. God help her, she wanted to say yes.

"I don't think it's going to take that long for things to return to normal," Pres told her. "Not with the statement I gave the press today."

"I have work to do, today, right now," Molly insisted. Why did he have to look so incredibly good, sitting there across from her in his expensive hand-tailored suit? His smile softened the hard lines of his face and his eyes made promises that were much too tempting.

"I have to clean all those bedrooms." She was reaching for an excuse now, and the look in his hazel eyes told her he knew it. But still she kept talking, hoping she'd hit on something that would ring true. "I want to get the place up and running by September, you know. That roofer—Emerson James—he's supposed to come by tomorrow morning. And I just...can't. Pres, I can't. I'm sorry. I hate the thought of being driven out of my home by a pack of...*idiots*."

Pres was watching her, his expression unreadable. But then he nodded. "You're right." He turned and nudged Zander's sneaker with the toe of one perfectly polished shoe. "She's right, you know. You should never let yourself get pushed around—especially not by idiots."

Zander didn't look convinced.

"You can stay at the resort as my guest some other time," he promised the boy. "But right now your mom wants to go home." He pressed the intercom button. "Kirk Estate, Lenny. On the double."

SEVEN

BAD THINGS always came in threes.

As the phone rang Pres braced himself for the third bad thing.

The first had been Molly refusing to come and stay at the resort.

Oh, he'd had that all planned out. They would order an elegant, gourmet room-service dinner and eat it on the living-room rug, spread out like a picnic. Then they'd rent a movie from the in-house video service, and around nine o'clock, they'd tuck a sleepy Zander into one of the king-size beds in the two-bedroom Presidential Suite.

Then he and Molly would wander out onto the screened-in balcony and...

Pres wanted to kiss her. Desperately. In fact, he was starting to obsess about it. The way her lips would feel. The way she would taste...God, it was driving him out of his mind.

Forget about his craving for cigarettes. That was nothing compared with how much he wanted Molly.

Instead, he'd driven her back to the Kirk Estate, made her promise to stay inside, told her a security team was already on the way, ready to keep unwanted visitors off her property throughout the night. And after the team had arrived, he'd left.

Pres picked up the phone. "Seaholm."

"Yeah, Pres. It's Mac. Sorry to disturb you, but we've got a problem." It was his security chief, calling from Molly's house with what had to be the third bad thing.

The second bad thing had been a message waiting for Pres on his answering machine when he got home. Randy, the owner of the salvage company down in St. John had called. There had been another major storm in the Virgin Islands that morning, and the shipwreck had been covered back up with sand. The location was marked, but instead of a comparatively quick and easy excavation, the endeavor would now be costly, dangerous, and time-consuming.

"Did something happen?" Pres asked Mac. "Are the Cassidys okay?"

"Everyone's fine," Mac told him. "My problem is this place is too big to patrol with only three men. I know you want someone inside the house at all times, but that means I've only got two guys outside and . . ." Pres could picture the big, burly former U.S. Navy SEAL shaking his head. "If someone really wants to, they're going to get past us."

"How many more men do you need?"

"At least two. But my staff is tapped out. Everyone's been working double shifts, handling this *Fantasy Man* thing. The fact is, Pres, I don't have anyone else left to call. And no way am I triple shifting. But I figured if anyone could pull a couple of guys out of his hat at eleven o'clock at night, it had to be you."

Pres smiled. His third bad thing just might've been a good thing after all. "I'll have two men—

fresh and ready to work—over at the Kirk Estate in ten minutes," he told Mac.

He hung up, then lifted the phone again, pressing the speed dial for Dominic's home number.

Molly looked up from the television news as the security guard checked his watch, stood up, and stretched.

"Shift change," he told her, crossing toward the French doors that led to the back patio.

As he went out another man came inside. He was dressed in similar black jeans and black T-shirt, and he wore a black baseball cap on his head. Molly barely glanced up at him. "There's coffee in the kitchen. Help yourself."

"I will, thanks."

The familiar voice got her full attention. It was Pres.

It was *Pres*?

Molly turned off the TV and followed him into the kitchen. "What are *you* doing here?"

"My security chief was low on manpower tonight." He tossed his cap onto the counter, then poured himself a mug of coffee. "Dom and I came over to help out."

Molly didn't want to be glad to see him. But, dammit, every time he showed up, her heart beat with a new, powerful, exciting rhythm. He knew it too. He knew it, and he was purposely making this as hard as possible for her. Molly tried to get mad, but she couldn't even do that. Not after what she'd just seen on the television.

"I saw you on the news," she said. "Today at the church—you told those reporters the truth."

He'd made a statement, admitted that he'd invented his engagement in order to get out of being *Fantasy Man*'s Most Eligible Bachelor of the Year. He'd told the world that Molly Cassidy was not his mysterious fiancée, because he *had* no fiancée.

"I want you and Zander to be left alone." Pres took a sip of his coffee, watching her evenly over the top of his coffee mug. Lord, he looked incredibly good in black.

"But you made the story up in the first place so that *you'd* be left alone."

He shrugged. "My priorities have changed."

Meaning her and Zander's privacy was now more important to Pres than his own. Molly crossed her arms and leaned back against the counter, hoping he wouldn't notice that she wasn't as cool and calm as she was pretending to be. "That's very sweet, but...I don't think anyone believed you."

He froze, his mug poised at his lips. "Why not?"

"A photographer was up on the roof of Millie's Market," Molly said. "After we came out into the alley...There's a picture...."

After they'd come out into that alley, he'd held her loosely in his arms and gazed down into her eyes and...

He was looking at her exactly that same way right now, with volcanic heat making his eyes a blistering swirl of green and yellow and brown.

"I didn't kiss you," Pres said.

"I know. But in the picture...They showed it on the news." Molly swallowed. "It looked like..."

"I wanted to kiss you."

Molly's eyes were wide. She looked about as old as Zander. "Yeah." She nervously moistened her lips and tried to smile. "That's sure what it looked like in that picture."

"No." Pres put down his coffee mug. "That's not what it *looked like*—that's what it was. I wanted to kiss you." He gave her a half smile. "I still do. Want to kiss you."

Molly stared at him, and Pres stared back at her, wondering what she was going to say, how she was going to respond.

She turned away from him suddenly, reaching for a mug and pouring herself some coffee. She wasn't going to say anything. Pres was disappointed. She'd been so honest about nearly everything else up to this point.

But then she turned back to him. "I know," she said, breaking the silence. "I want to kiss you too."

She took her coffee and walked out of the room.

"Whoa." Pres nearly tripped over his own feet in his haste to follow her. "Hold on a minute! Molly! Wait a sec.... You can't just say that you want to kiss me and then walk away."

She turned to face him. "I *don't* want to kiss you."

"But you just said..."

"I want to and I *don't* want to. Can you see

how that might be something of a problem for me?"

"Can't we maybe give it a trial run and see? If you still feel undecided afterward—"

Molly's cheeks were flushed and her eyes were hot. "Do you honestly think that either one of us will still have our clothes on after you start kissing me? Because I don't. I know damn well that one kiss will lead to two, and two will lead to... Lord! Before either of us knows it, we'll be up in my bedroom, making love."

"Um," Pres said.

"And don't pretend that's not exactly what you want," she blazed. "I know because I want it too. And I *don't* want it!" Her coffee sloshed over the top of the mug and burned her fingers. "Shoot! *Shoot!*" She put her fingers in her mouth trying to cool them.

Pres took her mug and set it down on the coffee table, then gently touched her burned hand, tugging her back toward the kitchen. "Maybe we should run this under cold water." He laughed. "Hell, maybe we should run *me* under cold water as well—"

Molly yanked her hand away from him. "Stop being so damned nice!"

"Actually, I wasn't being nice. Actually, I was just trying to get close enough to do this...."

Pres kissed her.

She tasted hot and sweet, like coffee, and she made a faint sound in the back of her throat as he deepened the kiss. Her lips were as soft as he'd imagined—softer.

He was just about to pull back when she reached for him, putting her arms around his neck, pulling him closer, startling him with her intensity as she returned his kisses.

She was an inferno. She was incredible. Pres would have laughed aloud if he hadn't been otherwise engaged.

Her breasts were deliciously soft against his chest, her stomach tight against his growing arousal. Her hair felt like silk beneath his fingers. Her tongue met his in an onslaught of passion so fierce, he was nearly knocked over.

He could feel her hands move down, down and underneath the edge of his T-shirt, her fingers cool against his bare skin.

She was right. If he had anything to say about

it—and he hoped to God that he did—they were going to make love, right here, right now.

"Mac wants to talk to you, Pres—oops."

Pres lifted his head to see Dom standing in the open French doors on the other side of the room.

"No, he doesn't," Pres said.

"No, he doesn't," Dom agreed, closing the door behind him.

"Oh, Lord." Molly brought her fingers to her lips. She was still pressed against him, and as she moved, Pres knew she couldn't have missed noticing how totally turned on he was. "Oh, Lord," she said again.

"We still have our clothes on," Pres felt it necessary to point out.

"Only because your friend came to the door."

"Remind me to fire him." Pres bent his head to kiss her again.

She tried to pull away. "Don't!"

He didn't let her go. "How could you not want to do that again? That was . . ."

"What?"

Pres was suddenly extremely aware that whether or not he was going to get this woman into bed with him tonight depended greatly on the word he used to describe that kiss. If he said the right thing, he just might have a chance. A very tiny chance, but it was his only chance.

And God, he wanted to make love to her so much.... He couldn't speak. He couldn't even think.

Awesome. Amazing. Incredible. Mind-blowing. Excellent. Transcendental. Blood-stirring. None of those were the right words.

How would *Molly* describe that kiss? What words would *she* use?

But that was a mistake. By trying to second-guess her, his words would ring false. It would get him nowhere.

And then he knew.

Just that morning, on the beach, Zander had taught him a sign. And wrong or right, it was the only word Pres could use to describe the kiss he and Molly had just shared.

He released her and held up the index finger on his left hand. He took hold of that finger with his thumb and index finger of his right hand and slowly lifted both hands.

"Unique," he whispered.

Molly laughed, a wonder-filled burst of air that

contradicted the sudden sheen of tears in her eyes. "That's today's word."

"It sure as hell is." Pres reached for her.

She let him pull her close, but she shook her head. "This is crazy...."

It was. It was incredibly crazy. For her sake, he was supposed to stay away from her, not be doing his damnedest to ensure that he woke up next to her in her bed.

But her eyes were a liquid shade of blue and she felt so right in his arms. And that kiss had truly been one of a kind. He could only imagine what making love to this woman would be like. And, oh, could he ever imagine it....

This was not the time to turn and walk away.

Her lips parted slightly as she gazed up into his eyes and he couldn't have stopped himself if he tried. He kissed her again, and she melted against him, and he felt a surge of triumph and desire. He'd won.

Her room was upstairs, he knew that much. He swept her up into his arms and ...

She heard the voices from out in the yard at the exact moment he did. Shouting. Mac's low baritone rasping out orders. The sound of running feet, and then tires, squealing, as a car raced away into the night.

Molly slid to the ground and Pres started for the door. It opened before he reached it, and Dom stepped inside.

"He got away," he said without introduction. "Some kind of photographer. Sonuvabitch was on the roof. Mac got the guy's camera, but when he checked, the film was gone."

On the roof.

Molly looked up, and Pres followed her gaze.

In that part of the big living room, the ceiling was raised and beams were exposed. And several big skylights had been cut into the roof—the result of renovations done to the old house some time in the late 1970s.

On the roof. Photographer.

One of those skylights was less than ten feet from where they had been standing when Pres had kissed Molly.

On the roof. Photographer. Film was gone.

A photograph where Pres only looked as if he wanted to kiss Molly had created a giant stir. He didn't want to guess at the public reaction to a photo of him actually kissing her.

But Dom was looking up at the skylight too. And he predicted the outcome of such a picture succinctly.

"You, my friend," Dom told Pres, "are in extremely deep doo-doo."

Molly woke up with a headache.

The sky was clear and blue, and for the first time in days the mugginess was gone. But she lay for a moment in her bed, wishing with all of her might that she didn't have to get up.

But Zander was already awake. She could hear their boom box playing loudly in the kitchen, blasting the soundtrack from the latest Disney movie release.

She struggled out of bed, throwing on her robe as she shuffled toward the bathroom. Her foot hit the morning newspaper. Zander must have brought it up to her room.

Suddenly horribly curious, Molly opened the paper, flipping quickly to the lifestyles section. Sure enough, an enormous picture of her and Pres, in a clinch steamy enough to bedeck the cover of the spiciest of romance novels was on the front page.

Nothing going on here, read the caption under the photo, *or so claims Preston Seaholm, real-estate tycoon and* Fantasy Man's *Most Eligible Bachelor of the Year, pictured above with his current lady love, Molly Cassidy.*

The *Sun Times* gossip columnist had a thing or two to say about the so-called affair too. *What's all the noise about Sunrise Key billionaire Preston Seaholm's latest romance? The man's illustrious title from* Fantasy Man *magazine isn't really that big a deal. And his divorce from overnight sensation Merrilee Fender is ancient history. So why all the attention? Because Pres Seaholm is making it so much fun, that's why. It's a mystery, it's a challenge, it's caught the attention of the American public.*

With all his wealth and prestige, the article continued, *Pres Seaholm is American royalty. He's the crown prince and unofficial spokesman for the classic American Dream.*

And he's so obviously hiding something.

First he says he's getting married, then withholds his fiancée's name. Then he denies that

Molly Cassidy is his bride-to-be, she's just a business associate, little more than an acquaintance. Then he claims he's not really getting married at all—he made the whole thing up.

This morning's photo shows Pres with his acquaintance, Molly Cassidy. Nothing's going on, indeed.

Molly's eyes were drawn back to the photo, to that incredible moment of passion and desire that had somehow been captured on film. She could still feel the power and strength of Pres's arms as he pulled her against him. She could still taste the heat of his kiss.

She would have slept with him. If they hadn't been interrupted, she would have willingly let him take her upstairs and . . .

Molly closed the newspaper, trying to push away the sudden heat that had flooded through her at the thought of taking Pres Seaholm to bed. As much as she'd wanted him last night, as much as she *still* wanted him, God help her, she knew it would be an incredible mistake.

She reached for the telephone, searching through the pile of papers on her bedside table, looking for the business card Pres had given her several days ago. She dialed his home number.

"'Lo?" He sounded as if...

"I woke you up."

"Molly?" She heard rustling sounds as if he were rolling over and sitting up. "Yeah, but that's okay. Is something wrong?" His voice was raspy and he cleared his throat.

"I'm sorry," she said, suddenly dreadfully nervous, suddenly painfully aware of the way his voice made her stomach tighten in anticipation. "I can call you later."

"No, I should've been awake. I'm awake now and... God, I need a cigarette. You're calling because you saw the morning paper. I was faxed a copy of the picture a couple of hours ago. It's... powerful."

"Yeah." She took a deep breath. "We need to talk."

"Give me about half an hour, and I'll come over."

Molly glanced at the clock. "Actually, Z has speech therapy this morning. The therapist's coming by in about an hour—his name's Hayden Young, do you know him?"

"You mean the guy who works as the lifeguard over at the town beach?"

"Yeah. He's really nice, and he doesn't mind if I take off for a couple hours while he works with Zander. I thought it might be more convenient for you if I came to your place."

"No, that's not a good idea. I'll come to you."

"I don't mind going out there if you'll just give me directions and—"

"Really," he said a touch too forcefully. "It's all right. I'll be over in a little while."

"Okay. Why don't you want me to see where you live?" Molly asked bluntly.

He was silent for a moment. Then he laughed. "Because nobody comes into my bungalow."

"Nobody?" She was intrigued. "Nobody except your cleaning lady, you mean."

"Nobody," he repeated. "Not the cleaning lady. Not Dominic. Nobody. You see, I don't get much privacy and—"

"You don't have to explain," she said quietly.

"It just . . . it sounds weird, but it's *my* mess, you know? Here in my bungalow, I can hang whatever pictures I want on the walls without having someone psychoanalyze 'em. My furniture doesn't have to match. I get so tired of everything in my life being perfectly color-coordinated."

Molly laughed. "You're right. It sounds very weird. But I won't tell anyone."

"Thanks. It's stupid, but it's important to me."

"If it's important to you, then it's not stupid," Molly told him. "Just come over whenever you're ready. I'll be here."

E I G H T

THE KIRK ESTATE was in an uproar.

Happy, cheerful, dauntless Zander was in tears, crying noisily as if the world were coming to an end.

From the kitchen came the jet-engine sound of a hair dryer.

And Molly stood with the telephone cord stretched as far as it could go from both noises, one finger plugged into her ear as she talked on the phone. Her face was tight, her shoulders tense.

She spotted Pres at the door and waved him

inside, but then turned her attention immediately back to the phone call.

Zander was lying facedown on the couch, sobs racking his skinny body. He was wearing only a bathing suit and both it and his hair were wet.

"What happened?" Pres asked.

The boy lifted his head. "I forgot I had my hearing aids on and I jumped into the swimming pool and now they're ruined and I won't be able to hear anything at school and I'm supposed to start on Monday because spring vacation's almost over and Mom didn't shout at me but I know that she wanted to and—"

As Zander drew in a breath Pres stopped him. "Whoa." He held out his hand to the boy. "Why don't we go outside so you can get some air?"

Zander nodded, his lower lip still trembling, tears still flowing.

It was hot outside, but a breeze was coming in off the Gulf, and it carried with it a cooling freshness. Pres sat down on the porch steps, and Zander sat next to him, hugging his knees into his chest, wiping his nose on his arm.

"You want to start at the beginning?" Pres asked the boy.

"I wasn't thinking," Zander said. "I wore my hearing aids into the pool." His eyes filled with a fresh flood of tears. "I'm not supposed to get them wet. I'm supposed to be careful even when it rains, and now I wrecked them."

"I didn't realize they were that fragile," Pres said.

Zander wasn't wearing his glasses and he scrubbed at his eyes. "They're like teeny sound systems. They have a little microphone and all kind of tiny electronic things that take the sounds I can't hear well and make them louder." He looked miserably up at Pres. "They were really, really, *really* expensive—more than seven hundred dollars *each*. And Mom's worried about money right now. I know we can't afford to buy new ones, but how can I go to school without them?"

Pres was shocked. He kept his face expressionless as he gazed out at the lush grounds of the estate. He realized he'd had absolutely no idea of Molly's financial situation. He'd assumed that Chuck Cassidy's widow would be rather well off, but if an unexpected fourteen-hundred-dollar expense could break them...

He looked over at Zander, nudging the boy with his elbow so he'd look up at his lips. "School starts Monday, huh?"

Zander nodded glumly. "Without my hearing aids, I might as well stay home."

"We'll figure something out, okay?" Pres told him.

The boy didn't look convinced.

Inside the house, the sound of the hair dryer shut off. Pres stood up. "I'm going to go talk to Molly, okay?"

Miserably, Zander nodded.

Pres went up the stairs, but before he could open the door, Molly came outside, holding the door open for Hayden Young, who was several steps behind her.

Hayden Young would've been the most hated man on Sunrise Key if it weren't for the fact that he was quite possibly the nicest man on Sunrise Key.

With the height and build of a professional football player, chiseled features in a ruggedly handsome face, and long, flowing blond hair, the town lifeguard had nearly every unattached woman in town lined up to take his CPR classes.

And here he was, coming over to Molly's house to work one-on-one with her son. Pres tried not to be jealous. And failed.

"I think I got them dried out," Hayden said to Zander with a smile, holding out the pair of hearing aids.

Molly glanced almost nervously at Pres. "I spoke to the hearing-aid distributor over on the mainland," she told her son, watching as he put his hearing aids into his ears. "She said that this model is made especially for children, and sometimes children jump into swimming pools. She thought they'd probably be fine, but we should go into the store this afternoon to make sure they're working right."

"I'm sorry," Zander said. He snapped his fingers, turning his head this way and that. "They *seem* okay...."

Molly knelt and hugged him. "We'll get them checked." She kissed the top of his damp head. "If we need to get you new ones, we'll get you new ones, all right?"

He nodded, still subdued.

"Come on, let's go inside," Hayden said to the boy. "We've got some work to do."

He held the door open for Zander, closing it tightly behind them both.

The sweet scent of the lifeguard's sun lotion seemed to linger in the air. Pres turned to look at Molly. "I didn't know Young was a speech therapist. Does he, uh, come out here often?"

"About three times a week. But when classes start again after vacation, he'll meet with Zander over at the school." She sat down tiredly on the steps. Pres sat next to her, and she tried to smile. "That was an exhausting fifteen minutes of chaos."

Her eyes filled with tears that she tried to hide from him. Pres thought about pretending that he didn't notice, but he couldn't stop himself from asking, "Are you okay?"

"I handled that all wrong," she admitted, not meeting his eyes. "I was so upset; but Zander was upset too. I should have paid more attention to him. But all I could think of were those damned hearing aids, and what we were going to do if they were seriously damaged." She looked up at him. "Thank you so much for talking to him and calming him down."

"If I ask you something that's maybe a little bit

personal and private, will you answer me honestly?"

"Of course." She looked at him and managed a rueful smile. "*I'm* not the one who lied to ten million people about being engaged."

Pres smiled too. "Oh, what a tangled web we weave, et cetera, et cetera. That little lie's probably going to haunt me the rest of my life, isn't it?"

"Just as long as it doesn't haunt *me* . . ." She took a deep breath and raked her hair back from her face with her fingers. "Okay. Go ahead. Ask me this awful question that I have to answer honestly. I'm ready."

"Before you inherited the Kirk Estate, where exactly did you and Zander live?"

Molly gave him an incredulous look. "That's your personal and private question?"

He nodded. "Yeah."

"We lived in Katonah—a suburb of New York City."

Pres nodded again. "I asked where *exactly*. Did you own a house? Do you still own a house there?"

Molly ran her tongue across her teeth. "Ah,"

she said. "This is where we get to the personal and private part, huh?"

Pres just waited for her answer.

"We lived in a ridiculously small two-bedroom apartment in the basement of a two-family house. Chuck had his typewriter set up in our bedroom and he worked—or rather stared at his keyboard—all hours of the day and night. Most nights I ended up sleeping on the living-room couch."

Pres leaned forward. "You lived there even when Chuck was alive? But I thought—" He stopped himself.

She gazed out at the yard. Her voice was matter-of-fact as she answered his unspoken question. "Right after we were married, right before Zander was born, Chuck made some really bad investments. He lost everything." She turned to look at him. "That's what you wanted to know, right?"

Her normally sparkling blue eyes were sharp with bitterness and her soft lips were a tight, grim line.

"You want to ask me about Chuck's mistress too?" she asked.

Molly had shocked Pres. She could see from the look on his face that this was that last thing he'd expected her to say.

But somehow he managed to hold her gaze. And his voice sounded so gentle when he spoke. "Do you want to tell me about Chuck's mistress?"

Silently, she shook her head no. And then she nodded yes. "In some ways it's not really as awful as it sounds. In others, it's worse. He was brilliant, you know? His stories were"—she shook her head—"beyond compare. I met him when I was doing an interview for my college newspaper. He wasn't a very talkative man—in fact, he was practically silent. And that added so much mystery to him. I had this fantasy of marrying him and having him finally *talk* to me. I wanted to know what he was thinking, I wanted to get inside his head."

She leaned her head back against the stair railing, briefly closing her eyes. Pres just waited for her to continue.

"So I married him. But he never really talked to me—not the way I wanted him to." She took a deep breath. "And then, after he died, his agent called me and said Chuck's editor needed my permission to publish a collection of letters. I didn't know what he was talking about, so they sent me a copy of over four hundred letters—*four hundred* letters—that Chuck had written to a woman who lived in Paris. She was married to a friend of his and...I guess he must've loved her. He never actually slept with her, but I can't think of her as anything but his mistress. He loved her. He wrote to her for years—starting before we were married and continuing right up until he died. Those letters contained all of his thoughts and dreams. They were what I'd wanted from him for all those years we were married. Instead, he talked to me about the laundry and what to have for dinner and which bills absolutely needed to be paid. After nearly seven years, we were still strangers. I was really nothing more than live-in domestic and nursing help. I worked two jobs just to pay the bills and he didn't even make his own damned lunch."

She shook her head. "I don't mean to sound so bitter and awful. The truth is, I really wouldn't have minded so much if he'd shared even just a *little* bit of himself with me. I wanted to know his soul, his essence, his intellect. But he gave that to someone else."

"Molly, why did you stay with him?"

"Because I loved him." She looked up to find Pres watching her. "At least I did at the beginning. I was only nineteen when I married him. He was so . . ." She glanced away, embarrassed.

"He was what?"

"He was a lot like you."

Pres was silent, and Molly tried to explain.

"He was rich and powerful and famous. He was perfect."

"I'm not perfect."

"*Fantasy Man* magazine thinks you are."

Pres snorted.

"And they're right," Molly insisted. "Look at you. Gorgeous hair, perfect teeth, that body . . . *And* you're sweet and generous and funny. No, you're definitely perfect."

He leaned back, resting his elbows on the step above them. "If I'm so perfect, why did you call me this morning and ask me to meet with you so you could give me a standard letdown speech?"

Molly shifted uncomfortably, and Pres knew he'd read her phone call correctly.

"That kiss last night was a mistake, right?" he continued. "Things got out of control. Wherever we were heading—it's not going to happen. You don't want to be anything more than friends. What else? Did I leave something out?"

"No, you touched on everything."

Pres nodded. "Everything but the reason why. I thought you just said I was perfect."

"I don't want perfect," she said quietly. "I'm sorry. But I do hope we can be friends."

Pres felt a surge of frustration. Damn, he needed a cigarette. He was dizzy and nauseated and exhausted and disappointed as all hell. He didn't want to be friends with this woman. He wanted to kiss her the way he'd kissed her last night. He wanted to carry her up to her bedroom and bury himself inside of her. He wanted to make love to her, nonstop, for two weeks.

But she wanted to be friends.

"I don't know if I can just be friends with you," he admitted. He lowered his voice. "I want to be your lover, Molly."

Her cheeks flushed and she looked away.

"I'm not Chuck," he persisted.

She finally looked up at him. "I know that."

"Then why are you pushing me away as if I were?"

She couldn't—or wouldn't—answer. Pres resisted the urge both to search frantically through his pockets for a cigarette and to scream. He stood up. "I'm sorry about last night—the picture in the paper, I mean. Not the kiss. I'm not sorry about that." He took a deep breath. "I'll keep a security team over here until things die down."

Molly nodded. "Thanks."

Pres made himself walk away. He walked around the side of the house, turning the corner that would bring him toward the front, but then stopped short.

There were half a dozen TV vans waiting out by the front gate, near where his car was parked. He quickly started to duck behind a shrub bedecked with cloyingly sweet flowers, but he was too late. They'd already spotted him.

He braced himself for the onslaught and headed toward his car, ignoring the questions and shouts of his name.

Hating every moment of it, he stopped next to his car and waited for a half-dozen microphones to be shoved into his face.

"I'd like to take this opportunity to repeat the statement I made last night," he said. "I wasn't telling the truth when, several days ago, I said I was engaged to be married. I was hoping you all would believe me and just go home and leave me alone.

"Ms. Cassidy is not and has never been my fiancée. Yes, I find her incredibly attractive. Yes, I've kissed her—you've all seen proof of that. But the fact is, Molly Cassidy and I are nothing more than friends."

Pres turned away and got into his car. He'd told them the truth, but this time he honestly wished it were another lie.

Pres left his office well after six and nearly ran directly into Hayden Young in the resort lobby.

"Hey, Pres, what's up?" the bigger man said cheerfully.

"What brings you out this way?" Pres crossed his arms, trying to squelch the slow burn of jealousy he felt. Hayden had stayed at the Kirk Estate long after Pres had left there that afternoon. Hayden would be going back next week, to work with Zander. Hayden would see Molly too—she'd probably smile at him as she opened the door and welcomed him into her home. Hayden was one lucky sonuvabitch. But with his cheerful smile and serene, easygoing attitude, the man was impossible to dislike.

"My parents are down on the key for a visit," Hayden told Pres. "They're staying here at the resort. We're having dinner in just a few minutes at your restaurant. Tell the chef to go wild."

"I will." Pres paused. "How'd the speech session go with Zander today?"

Hayden made a so-so motion with his hands. "The kid was tense about a lot of things: getting his hearing aids wet, all those reporters outside his house.... None of that helped. And school starts next week—he's going to be the new kid. That's got to be scary for him. New friends to make, new teacher to deal with . . . I didn't feel like I had his full attention all afternoon. In fact, we ended early today."

"What exactly do you do with him?"

"Mouth-and-tongue-placement exercises. It's not easy for him. Can you imagine having to learn to make a sound that you can barely hear? *S, sh, f, th*. They all sound the same to him. The kid's doing really well, considering." Hayden grinned. "Of course, the fact that he talks *all* the time means he gets a lot of practice."

Pres smiled. "Yeah, Zander does make for a lively conversation."

"Most of the time he works hard. He seems to have a really good understanding of the fact that it's important for him to learn to speak clearly now, while he still has some hearing."

Pres felt a chill in the pit of his stomach. "While he still has some hearing?"

"Zander's condition is degenerative." Hayden looked puzzled. "Didn't Molly tell you?"

Pres could barely breathe. *Degenerative*. "No."

Hayden shook his head and backed away slightly. "I shouldn't be talking to you about this, then. I'm sorry, I thought you knew. I mean, it's no big secret, but I feel funny discussing it if—"

"Degenerative as in Zander's hearing is getting worse?" Pres asked. He knew that's exactly what it meant, but he needed it spelled out.

Hayden nodded. "Yeah," he said, compassion darkening his expressive blue eyes. "Tough break, huh? All signs indicate that the kid's going to be profoundly deaf by the time he's twenty years old."

Pres felt sick. Zander was going to be *profoundly* deaf. Suddenly it all made sense. The sign language, the word a day, the music. Molly and Zander listened to a new CD every single day—because in a few short years Zander wasn't going to be able to hear music anymore.

I wish I could be an opera singer when I grow up, the boy had told Pres. *I love music more than anything in the world.*

Pres felt tears stinging hotly against his eyes. "Oh, God."

"Zander's actually pretty lucky," Hayden said.

"Lucky?"

"A degenerative hearing condition can be really tough to deal with. Most people don't have the kind of support Zander gets from Molly."

Molly. How could she stand it? How could she be so optimistic and happy when her beautiful son was losing his hearing bit by bit, piece by piece, a little more each day? Who, Pres wondered, was supporting Molly?

How did she handle those long nights all alone, while Zander was fast asleep? Did she mourn quietly, or angrily curse out the fates for making her child walk this path? Did she try to strike a deal with the Creator, offering him everything and anything in return for her son's precious hearing?

And Pres knew in a sudden flash that he had found Molly's price. He knew without a doubt that she would sell him the Kirk Estate in a heartbeat if he could offer her a way to restore Zander's hearing.

There had to be some kind of operation or medical technique that was revolutionary and probably outrageously expensive. But outrageously expensive wouldn't stop Preston. Not when it came to Zander. Or Molly.

Forget about buying the house. The house was nothing. It was insignificant. It no longer mattered.

What mattered was Zander. And Molly.

"Excuse me," Pres said to Hayden, turning away.

Dom was still at the front desk, waiting for the evening shift to arrive, but Pres walked right past him, heading out to the back lot where his truck was parked.

The *American Lifestyles* van was lying in wait, and Pres knew it would follow him all the way to Molly's.

But for once, he didn't give a damn.

NINE

"I CAN'T BELIEVE you didn't tell me!"

"It didn't come up."

Pres lowered his voice, aware of the sound of music drifting downstairs from Zander's room. "Zander's going to be totally deaf in less than ten years, and it *didn't come up*?"

"It's not as if we've had that many conversations," Molly pointed out. "And it's not something I usually mention upon introduction: Hi, how are you, I'm Molly Cassidy and this is my son, Alexander, who's hearing-impaired with a degenerative condition that will render him profoundly deaf sometime within the next decade."

Pres closed his eyes and rubbed his forehead. "You're right. I'm sorry. It's just . . . I wish you had told me."

"There's a chance the degeneration will halt," Molly said, lifting her chin. "It's not likely, but there have been other cases where—"

"What are the odds of that happening?"

She looked away from him. "Slim to none."

"And still you hope." There was such wonder in his voice.

"Of course I hope." Molly looked up at him, but had to look away again. The sad gentleness in his eyes was too much to bear. She cleared her throat, trying not to cry. "And even though I hope, we prepare for the worst."

Pres moved toward her, and she stepped back, away from the dangerous lure of his arms. He shouldn't have come here, screeching to a stop in the driveway as if he'd driven from the resort like a bat out of hell. A news van had followed him, and Molly knew they had gotten it all on tape— the way he'd run to the front door and pounded until she'd opened it.

If they wanted the news media to believe there was nothing between them, this wasn't the way to do it.

He shouldn't have come here, and above all else, he shouldn't take her in his arms and kiss her. She knew far too well that once they started, she wouldn't want to stop.

"I want to buy Zander a music collection," Pres told her. "I want to take him over to the mainland and have him pick out all the CDs he wants. All the Mozart and what's-his-name...?"

"Alan Menken."

"Right. And anything else he wants. The Beatles. Garth Brooks. Coolio. Anything."

But Molly was shaking her head. "That's too much. We couldn't accept that kind of gift."

"Why not?" He was standing there looking at her, wearing an expensive-looking turquoise polo shirt and beige shorts that had been hand-tailored to fit him disgustingly well. He was wearing that watch of his that had probably cost more than her used car. He didn't understand why they couldn't accept his gift. He honestly didn't get it.

"It's too much," Molly explained. "He's ten

years old, Pres. He wouldn't pick out just one or two CDs. He'd pick out two hundred. More."

"But that's the idea. Let him have what he wants. Hell, I'll buy him two thousand if he wants 'em."

"You're talking about spending tens of thousands of dollars!"

"So?"

"So? That's insane!"

"No, it's not. Molly, in ten years it'll be too late. Let me buy the CDs for him now. *Please.*"

"Can you imagine the field day those news-magazines will have when they find out you bought a twenty-thousand-dollar gift for my son?" Molly asked. "Pres, I can't let you do it."

His jaw tightened. "Screw the newsmagazines. Let 'em say what they want. Let 'em think we're getting married. I don't care anymore. I'm just going to say 'no comment' until they go away."

"That's easy for *you.* You didn't just spend the entire afternoon on the phone with the elementary-school principal trying to figure out what to do if these damned reporters follow Zander to school on Monday."

Pres froze. "Mother of God. I never thought of that. I'll . . . I'll go to school with him."

"Oh, that will really help him fit right in." Molly rolled her eyes in disgust. "Maybe all the kids will bring along their mothers' billionaire lovers."

"I'm not your lover. Although, believe me, I'd like to—"

"You, me, and Zander are the only three people in the world who know that you're not. The other forty-seven trillion—"

"Can think what they want. And I think you're wrong. I think a lot of people believed me when I said we weren't engaged or even involved." Pres smiled ruefully. "And they're all single and female and staying up at the resort."

Molly was temporarily distracted. "Really?"

He nodded. "There's been an incredible run on rooms."

"Poor baby," she said, snorting. "Must be tough with all those gorgeous, available women walking around the lobby in thong bikinis . . ."

"I hid in my office all afternoon. Now, if it had been you walking around the resort lobby in a thong bikini," he continued, "I would've come out of hiding."

"Me in a thong bikini?" Molly laughed. "Dream on, Seaholm."

"I will," he murmured. "I have been."

Molly felt her cheeks heat with a blush and she turned away. Pres must've realized he'd gone too far, because he brought the conversation back to safer ground.

"Well, what did Zander's principal suggest? What are we going to do to keep the media away from the school?" he asked.

We. Molly tried not to like the sound of that word too much. "I don't know. We have the weekend to come up with some kind of plan."

"Or to defuse the situation." Pres shook his head. "Molly, I truly feel awful about getting you and Zander involved in this."

"Maybe..." Molly said.

"What?"

She nervously chewed on the end of her hair. "This might be a really stupid idea, and I can't even believe I'm saying this out loud, but... Maybe we should just pretend that we're engaged."

Pres had to turn away. Pretend they were engaged. Oh, my God.

"You know," she continued with a crooked smile, uncertain as to his response. "Appear together in public. Let the press take lots of pictures of us together. Kill the mystique and intrigue and..." She watched him uncertainly. "Bad idea?"

For Pres and Molly to appear together in public as an engaged, loving couple was so utterly *not* a bad idea. Pres could barely contain himself, imagining the possibilities. Whether or not it would work to defuse the situation was a different story.

He kept his voice matter-of-fact, even managing to sound a little skeptical. "Maybe it's worth a try." Yes, yes, yes, *yes,* it was *definitely* worth a try.

"Do you think?"

Molly was looking at him with her blue eyes wide and hopeful. She was doing this for Zander, he realized. For Zander's sake, she would appear with Pres in public. She would share romantic, candlelit dinners, she would walk hand in hand with him on the beach, she would probably even kiss him.

God, he hoped so.

And then something flickered in Molly's eyes. Something tiny and nearly unnoticeable that made him wonder if just maybe a part of her was doing this because she wanted to.

Last night she'd told him that she wanted to kiss him, but she didn't want to kiss him.

This would take all decision making out of her hands. She would *have* to kiss him. For Zander's sake.

Pres didn't care what her reasons were. He just wanted her in his arms again.

"Let's try it," he said.

"Let me see if I got this straight. You want me to spend my Saturday night *babysitting*," Dom said. "The resort is filled with more excruciatingly beautiful women than it ever has been before, and you want me to spend the evening having burgers and root beer and playing video games in the arcade with a ten-year-old kid."

"Yes," Pres said. "Please?"

Dom crossed the plush carpeting of Pres's private suite and sat down on the sofa, watching through the door as Pres slipped on his jacket and adjusted his tie in the bedroom mirror. He raised his voice to be heard in the other room. "Just promise me that the kid's not a brat."

"The kid's not a brat. I swear. He's the sweetest kid I've ever met. You're gonna love him."

"Let's not go that far. I'll endure him. Because I know how badly you want this." Dom untied his bow tie with a single accomplished pull and unfastened the top few buttons of his shirt. "Hey— are you sure this isn't illegal? Me distracting the kid while you try to seduce the mother?"

Pres came out of the bedroom. "It's called babysitting, Dom. It's legal. And my goal tonight isn't to seduce Molly." He paused. "At least not exactly."

"Oh, good, then you'll be back before eleven?"

Pres ignored his friend. "I've booked them a room. Suite 314."

"Oh, so it *is* going to be a slumber party...."

"Molly'll tell you what time Zander should be in bed. Until then, knock yourself out. Let him order room service, whatever he wants...."

"What if it's pizza and beer?"

"Whatever he wants within reason."

"I know," Dom said, a grin lighting his craggy face. "I'm just jerking you around."

Pres gave himself one last look in the foyer mirror. He'd suffered long over what to wear to this dinner date with Molly. He didn't want to wear a suit and be too formal. But shorts and a polo shirt were definitely not enough. He'd finally settled on a softly faded pair of stonewashed blue jeans, a crisp white shirt, lightweight sport jacket, and low-key tie. "How do I look?"

"Like the most eligible bachelor of the year," Dom told him. "Hearts are going to break tonight, my friend."

Pres nodded. "Keep your fingers crossed that mine's not one of them."

The elevator door was going to open in a matter of seconds. In a matter of seconds Molly and Preston were going to walk out of that elevator and into the resort lobby, where a dozen or more photographers were waiting to snap their picture.

"It'll be still photographers only," Pres

reminded her, giving her a reassuring smile. "No TV cameras, no questions. Just smile and . . . look like you like me."

Molly lunged forward and pulled the elevator stop button. "I'm not sure I can do this."

Lord, she was so nervous, she was nearly hyperventilating. Pres, on the other hand, looked so calm and cool. And gorgeous. The elevator light glinted off his golden hair, bringing out the hint of red. His eyes were a perfect mix of brown and green.

"It's not too late to back out," he said quietly.

"Yes, it is." Molly took a deep breath and looked at her reflection in the mirrored walls.

She looked . . . okay. Not half as good as Preston, but not as awful as she'd thought she'd look while she was pawing through her closet, searching desperately for something to wear. She'd finally found this blue sundress. It was simple, with a basic sleeveless bodice and a long, graceful skirt. With her hair up off her neck, she thought she looked vaguely elegant.

"We'll go out there," Pres told her, "stand for a moment while they take our picture, and then we'll go into the dining room. We'll order drinks and appetizers, and then we'll get up to dance. We don't have to do it for long—just long enough to let the photographers get more pictures. Our dinner order will take priority over everything else coming out of the kitchen tonight, so we'll get our food quickly. We'll eat as much or as little of it as you like, and then we'll leave." He smiled at her. "Okay?"

Molly had to smile back at him. "I feel like I've just been briefed to go fight a crucial battle in a war. Are you sure we shouldn't synchronize watches?"

"You're not wearing a watch."

"Good point."

"This is going to be okay," Pres said.

Molly nodded and reached for the button to restart the elevator. But she didn't press it in. She pulled her hand away and turned to face him again.

"One more thing I'm a little nervous about that you didn't touch on in your briefing..."

Pres nodded. "Yes, I'm going to kiss you again."

"When? I mean, not to sound as if I need to know *exactly* when, but...If I did know exactly when, it might help me be a little bit less nervous and—"

"When we're dancing."

"Ah."

"And maybe when we're not dancing."

"Well, that just about covers it, doesn't it?"

"Maybe if I kiss you now, it'll relax you—"

Molly pushed in the button and the elevator started moving. "No, thanks. I'd like to arrive in the lobby with all my clothes on, please."

This time Pres leaned forward and pulled the stop button. "I almost forgot...." He took a small box from his pocket. "We have to make this look official." He handed the box to Molly.

It was a jeweler's box, small and hard and covered with the softest black velvet. Molly opened it slowly, afraid to look inside.

It was a ring, just as she'd expected. But not just any ring.

"Good Lord, it's the Hope Diamond."

Pres laughed. "No, it's not."

It was awful. Molly had never seen such a gaudily decorated ring in her life. "It's...certainly something, isn't it?" She glanced up at him.

"It's a Seaholm family heirloom," Pres told her.

"My grandmother wore it, and my mother after her."

It was enormous. It looked like one of those disgusting ring lollipops that Zander liked to eat.

"Don't you like it?"

"It's much too big," Molly said, trying hard to be diplomatic. "It'll catch on everything, and... what if I *lose* it?"

"It's big enough—it should be easy to find."

"It's big enough to use teeing off on the country-club golf course," Molly told him. "Besides, what if your mother wants it back?"

"She won't," Pres said. "She's not a Seaholm anymore. She remarried a few years ago, after my father died." He looked down at the ring. "So you *don't* like it?" He was trying hard not to smile, and Molly suddenly realized as he took another box from his pocket that he had been teasing her. "You were remarkably tactful." He took the box with the gaudy ring from her hands and replaced it with the other.

"So that *wasn't* a Seaholm family heirloom?"

"Actually, it was," he said with a smile. "But I figure as long as I was going to break family tradition by becoming engaged without getting married, I can ignore the family-heirloom engagement ring too."

Molly looked at the box in her hands. "I'm afraid to look inside this one."

Preston reached forward and opened it for her.

It was a sapphire. It was big, but not too big, and it sparkled and gleamed with a blue fire. The setting was simple, with only one small diamond adorning it.

Molly swallowed the lump in her throat. "Oh, wow..."

"I knew you'd like this one."

She glanced up at him. "What if I'd liked the other one?"

"Then I would have actually had to marry you," Pres said, his eyes dancing with amusement. "Because where else would I find a woman who honestly likes that ring—"

"There are probably a few hundred of them here at the resort right now."

"You didn't let me finish," he pointed out. "What I was going to say was, where else would I find a woman who likes that ring, and yet still maintains a sense of humor and some degree of good taste?" He motioned to the sapphire ring. "Try it on."

Molly took the ring from the box, then realized she still wore her wedding ring on her left hand. She was going to have to take that off.

She'd never taken it off. Ever. But she'd wanted to. After Chuck had died, when she read all those letters he'd written to someone else . . . Still, she'd kept the ring on. Out of what? A sense of loyalty? Or as a reminder to her of her poor judgment when it came to men and marriage?

She tugged at her ring, but it stuck on her knuckle.

"May I help?" Pres took her hand and eased the ring off. His hands were warm and so gentle. He took the sapphire ring from her, and slid it onto her finger.

It somehow seemed a far too intimate act and Molly gazed up at him, for a moment unable to breathe.

He put her wedding band into the ring box. "I'll hold this for you," he said quietly.

She nodded.

He seemed as aware of the intimacy of the moment as she was, and he forced a smile, trying to break the mood. "I feel like I should get down on my knees and beg you not to marry me."

"Don't worry—I would accept. I have no intention of marrying you."

"Promise?" he asked.

Molly felt her lips curve up into a smile, and they both laughed.

"With all my heart. Do *you* promise?"

"I do. Although I remain hopeful that we can celebrate our engagement with an early version of the honeymoon."

Molly started the elevator, pulling away from the heat in his eyes. He may have been teasing, but he was also dead serious. "Like I said before, dream on, Seaholm."

"And like *I* said, I will. I'm a big believer in dream and wish fulfillment."

The doors slid open.

Molly turned and looked at Pres, her eyes wide. This was it. Time to go. He held out his hand to her, and she grasped his fingers tightly.

Together they stepped out of the elevator.

TEN

A WALL OF flashbulbs went off, blinding Molly. Pres dropped her hand and put his arm around her shoulders.

"Smile," he breathed into her ear.

To her surprise, she *could* smile. In fact, she started to laugh. "This is crazy," she told him as the volley of flashes kept going.

"Hold up your left hand," he said into her ear. "Show 'em that ring."

She did, and another huge volley of pictures were taken.

Pres held her tightly, and she suddenly became

aware that she was pressed up against him, from her shoulders all the way down to her thighs. He stood slightly behind her, his chest against her back, her bottom nestled quite securely against his leg. She was going to dance with Pres tonight, and he was going to hold her this close. Except when he did, they would be face-to-face, body to body, heart to heart.

And then he was going to kiss her. He'd told her as much.

Molly tried to squelch the sudden feeling of anticipation that filled her. But she couldn't make it go away. She wanted Pres to kiss her. She wanted to taste the powerful heat of his desire again.

He touched her lightly, running his fingers down her bare arm, and she couldn't breathe. Lord, she was in big trouble here.

Pres felt Molly tremble and he held her tighter. "We're almost done," he said into her ear, trying to sound reassuring, trying not to let her hear how completely the softness of her body against his was throwing him.

"How many pictures are they going to take?" she wondered aloud.

"As many as we let them." Pres took her hand,

gently pulling her with him away from the photographers and toward the resort dining room.

"Are they going to follow us?" she asked.

"Most of them probably already have tables re-
served," Pres told her. "Of course, they can't use
flash attachments in the restaurant."

Molly glanced around, and Pres knew she was
looking at the elegant restaurant for the very first
time. "This is lovely," she murmured, and he had
to agree.

It looked particularly good tonight, all gleaming white linen tablecloths and candlelight. The
big glass windows that filled the entire westward-
facing wall captured the last streaks of the sunset,
presenting a softly faded red-orange panorama of
sky and clouds and ocean.

Dave Zigfield was the Saturday-night maître d',
and he was quietly elegant in his black tuxedo as
he showed them to their table by the dance floor.
Pres held out Molly's chair, then sat down next to
her.

"Champagne, please," Pres commanded. "The
best in the house." Zig quickly and quietly disappeared.

"The best champagne in the house," Molly

mused. "I should remember to become engaged to celebrity billionaires more often."

Zig appeared almost instantly with a champagne bottle cooling in a wine bucket, silently setting two paper-thin, tulip-shaped glasses in front of Pres and then nearly as quietly popping the cork.

Pres could hear the sound of a dozen camera shutters closing as he and Molly lifted their glasses in a silent toast.

"I feel like a fish in a fishbowl," she murmured, letting the sapphire ring catch the candlelight.

Pres let himself look at her. At first glance, her dress was rather plain. But on closer examination, it was clear that the pale blue color suited Molly, and the simple style proved the old adage that less is often more. The soft cotton nestled modestly around her curves, giving only a hint that the body underneath was utterly feminine. In some ways, it was far sexier than a tight-fitting, more revealing dress.

She glanced away from him, pink tingeing her cheeks. "Don't look at me like that."

He couldn't help himself. Her silky brown hair was drawn up in a sophisticated tangle on top of her head. Several tendrils escaped the clamplike device that was holding it all together, making her look even younger than she was. The effect was thoroughly charming. She wore but a trace of makeup, a bit of something on her eyes, some lipstick on her beautifully shaped lips. Mother of God, he wanted to kiss those lips again....

Pres pushed back his chair. "Let's dance."

"But we were going to order first—"

"Change in plans." He held out his hand. "Come on."

"But the band's not even playing...." Before she finished her sentence, the conductor lifted his baton, and a sixteen-piece swing band began a slow, familiar melody. She stared up at Pres. "They're playing 'Stardust.' That's my favorite song."

He smiled. "I know. Zander told me."

Molly had to laugh as she let him pull her up out of her chair. "You've gone to an awful lot of trouble for a charade. Finding out my favorite song, picking out this incredible ring...It seems almost a shame. All that effort wasted on a game of make-believe."

"It's not entirely make-believe. In case you haven't noticed, I'm trying to seduce you."

"You know, come to think of it, I *have* kind of noticed."

"How'm I doing?"

Molly shook her head. "I don't suppose you'd give up if I told you that you didn't stand a chance?"

"Give up? No way."

Pres drew her into his arms, easily, naturally, as if she belonged there, and for half a second she could almost believe that she did. He was as easy to dance with as he was to talk to. And he was remarkably easy to talk to. He was open and direct—at least when it came to talking about *her* problems and *her* secrets.

He'd yet to reveal any of his own.

And Molly knew he had his secrets. A man like Preston Seaholm *definitely* had secrets.

He lifted her chin, and lowered his mouth to hers, and then, dear Lord, he was kissing her. His mouth was so soft, his lips so gentle. It was a sweet kiss, a tender kiss, soft and slow and heart-breakingly romantic. It was so different from the all-consuming way he'd kissed her before, yet somehow it seared her just as completely.

He tasted of champagne, sweet and heady. Molly didn't want to stop kissing him.

He didn't want to stop, either, but he did. "God, lady, you get me going," he breathed in her ear, holding her even closer.

Molly could hear his heart pounding, beating a rhythm that was almost as crazy as her own.

"You stopped smoking." She had to say *something,* and it seemed curiously appropriate.

Pres nodded, his cheek smooth against hers. He must have shaved right before he met her for dinner. It seemed sweet and totally unnecessary, and it made Molly's heart flip-flop. When was the last time a man had gone to such trouble for her?

"I had my last real cigarette forty-six hours, seventeen minutes, and five seconds ago," he told her.

She pulled back to look into his eyes. She felt alarmingly light-headed. "Last *real* cigarette?"

"Last night I had just a couple of drags of—"

"Oh, Preston, that's cheating. Just because you don't have the whole thing doesn't make it less real. If you quit, you quit. No cheating," she admonished him. She gave him a long look. "You seem to be doing okay, cheating aside."

"It's killing me," Pres admitted. "I'm in serious agony."

"Don't be in agony on my account," Molly said. "Have a cigarette."

"No." He leaned forward, once again capturing her lips with his.

Molly felt herself melt as his tongue lazily explored her mouth. But just as quickly as he began kissing her, he pulled back. "The only time I'm not dying for a cigarette is when you kiss me," he whispered. "And that's because when you kiss me, I'm too busy dying for you even to think about smoking."

He lowered his head for another kiss, and Molly couldn't resist. She knew that his soft words were just that—soft words. But combined with his intoxicating kisses, they made her breathless and hopelessly off balance.

He kissed her harder now, deeper, longer, with an explosion of incendiary passion that made her cling to him. They'd long since given up all pretense of dancing. The other couples on the hardwood floor flowed around them as Pres kissed her again and again.

She was doing this for the photographers, she tried to convince herself. If it weren't for the fact that she and Pres had to make the photographers believe they were truly engaged to be married and deeply in love, she would never kiss anyone this way. Not in public.

"Molly, come back to my suite with me." Pres's voice was hoarse, his breathing ragged. He rested his forehead against hers. "Please?"

He'd asked her to his suite here at the resort. It was probably exactly like the room where Zander was hanging out, watching videotapes with Pres's friend Dominic. It was elegant, it was lavish, but it was impersonal and cold.

And the sad truth was, if Pres had asked her to his bungalow, if he'd invited her into the privacy of the place that was truly his home, she would have gone.

If he'd given her just a little bit of himself, she would have given him her heart.

But he hadn't. He'd offered her nothing but the false closeness of physical intimacy.

Molly fought her disappointment. She should

be grateful. She should be glad. She'd come dangerously close to getting in too deep with a man that she didn't even know—that she probably would never truly know.

"Come on, Molly," he pressured her softly. "Say yes. I swear you won't regret it."

Won't regret it? She already did.

"I can't, Pres," she whispered.

He gazed into her eyes, searching for something. Finally he nodded. And tried to smile. And began to dance with her again. "This doesn't mean I'm giving up, so don't get any ideas."

"We're nearly strangers," Molly said, feeling the need to explain. "You don't know even the most basic things about me. You don't know that I was an only child, that my mother died when I was in high school, that my dad still hasn't gotten over it. You don't know that my favorite color's blue, and that if provoked, I can eat an entire sleeve of Chips Ahoy in one afternoon." She paused, looking up at him. "And I don't know anything about you."

She hoped he would realize what she wanted from him—what she *needed* from him. Still, she knew it was a mistake to give him such strong hints. Not only did it go against everything she believed to play relationship guessing games, but she knew that she absolutely couldn't let herself fall for this man. She'd walked that road before. She couldn't take that kind of risk again.

"Okay," he said. "I was an only child too. My dad died about three years ago and Mom's remarried. *My* favorite colors are the colors of the beach—blue, green, and white. If provoked, I can smoke two packs of cigarettes a day."

Molly shook her head, trying to resist the urge to rest her head on his shoulder, trying to ignore the seductive sway of his body so close to hers.

"Not good enough," he guessed, loosening his hold on her just enough so that every time he moved, his thighs brushed hers. "So what else do you want to know?"

Her mouth was dry. It wasn't too late to change her mind and tell him yes, she'd go back to his suite with him. The look in his eyes told her he was hoping that she would.

She cleared her throat. "Everything. Anything. Tell me something that you've never told anyone else. Tell me one of your darkest, most horrible secrets."

Pres smiled at her, and she couldn't look away from the ocean-green swirl of his eyes. "I don't have any horrible secrets."

"Then why won't you talk to the reporters about Merrilee Fender?"

Something changed in his face. There was a flash of pain in his eyes that he quickly smiled to cover up. "Good point," he said, but he didn't explain.

Molly couldn't hold it in. "Oh my God, you still love her."

His laughter was half-incredulous, half-exasperated. "Don't be absurd."

"There's nothing absurd about it. She's beautiful and—"

"I *don't* still love her. The truth is, I never did."

Molly stared at him. There was obviously much more to this than he'd let on. And he was just as obviously not going to say anything more.

"Why are we talking about my ex-wife?" he asked. "Can we *please* stop talking about my ex-wife?"

Molly looked away, wondering why he had married a woman he didn't love. But she wanted him to tell her about it because he wanted to, not because she asked. "I'm sorry."

Pres lifted her chin. "*I'm* the one who should be apologizing. I didn't mean to sound so ... Can we just forget about Merrilee tonight?"

Molly nodded and smiled, but her blue eyes were so subdued. "Maybe we should order our dinner now," she said quietly.

As they walked back to the table Pres kept his hand lightly and possessively on her back. But it was all just part of the act. He knew damn well that despite the ring she wore on her finger, he didn't possess Molly Cassidy in any way, shape, or form. And as much as he wanted to make love to her, he also knew it wasn't going to happen tonight.

It might've happened. There was a moment on the dance floor when he'd kissed her and was sure he was heading straight for heaven. But then something had gone wrong.

Pres replayed their conversation over and over in his head, searching for something he might've said to offend, something he might've done. . . . Or maybe it was something that he *didn't* say. . . . But what?

As he held Molly's chair and sat down next to her at their table, as Zig came right over, dancing immediate attendance upon them, Pres realized that there was only one thing of which he was positive.

And that was that he didn't have a clue.

Dr. Marsh Devlin, the island's sole physician, was clearly confused. "So you're *not* here to have a blood test for your marriage license. . . ."

"Because the engagement's just a sham," Pres finished for him.

Marsh crossed his arms and sat on the edge of his desk. "I'm sorry to hear that," he said in his crisp English accent. "Molly Cassidy is a delightful woman. When I heard that you two were engaged, I thought . . ." He looked down at his own shining new gold wedding band on his left hand and smiled.

Pres lowered himself into one of the chairs across from Marsh's desk, stretching his legs out in front of him. "You thought what?"

"It's odd, actually," Marsh said, still staring at his ring. "This marriage thing. I can't explain it medically, but when you get married, something happens to your brain, and you get...well, slightly stupid, I think. You say 'I do,' and then you instantly want everyone else around you to say it, too, regardless of their situation. I mean, I'm sitting here thinking you're a fool for not actually going ahead and marrying this woman, when in reality *I'm* the fool. You surely have your reasons for doing what you're doing, right?"

Pres nodded, unable to hide a smile.

"And therefore I shouldn't feel bad or sorry for you because you're not going to do exactly what I did. And in fact, you *can't* do exactly what I did, because what I did was marry Leila, and I'd be damned upset if you attempted to do the same."

"How is Leila?"

Marsh smiled, his lean face relaxing. "Fabulous, thanks. Amazingly wonderful. Exquisitely excellent. You're sure you don't want a blood test?"

Pres laughed. "No thanks. Molly and I really are just pretending to be engaged. The whole thing started out as a little lie I told during a press conference. I didn't want to be *Fantasy Man*'s Most Eligible Bachelor of the Year, so I fibbed and told the news teams that I was going to get married. But someone had a picture of me with Molly, and one thing led to another. They didn't believe me when I told them I made it all up, so now we're seeing if the media attention will die down if we give them what they want. What we're really trying to do is keep those vultures away from Molly's son."

"I heard about what happened over at the church."

"Zander starts school tomorrow," Pres told the doctor. "I've issued invitations for our official engagement party to all those Peeping Tom–type shows that try to pass themselves off as news, like *American Lifestyles*. The party's on Wednesday night, up at the resort, eight o'clock—tell Leila and consider yourself invited."

"I will, thanks." Marsh shifted his weight, pushing himself more fully up onto his desk. "So let's get this straight: You're having a party to officially announce an engagement that's not really real?"

"I know, it's crazy. But I can't think of anything else to do. The main thing is that we've let these camera crews know that their attendance at this event depends on their leaving Zander alone—you know, not harassing him at school. If we get word that Zander's being followed or bothered in any way, they get scratched from the guest list."

"I hope it works."

Pres nodded. He did too.

"So if not a blood test, what are you here for?" Marsh asked.

"Information."

"Something to do with one of your scuba-diving projects?"

Pres shook his head. "No. I want to talk to you about Zander Cassidy."

Marsh stood up and crossed to the other side of his desk. "Pres, the boy's a patient. Without his mother's permission I can't discuss—"

"I'm not asking you to break any rules," Pres told him. "I know the kid has some kind of degenerative hearing loss. That's not a secret. I just want you to help me understand what that means, and what can be done to correct the situation."

Marsh sat down behind his desk. "If you have questions, I'm sure Molly could answer them—probably even better than I. Audiology is not my specialty, and she's done quite a bit of research—"

"It's kind of an emotional issue, and the fact is, Molly's not a doctor." Pres leaned forward. "Come on, Marsh. Tell me what this kid's prognosis is and what the options are for changing it. I care about these people. I want to know what I can do to help."

Marsh folded his hands on his desk and levelly met Pres's gaze. "Alexander Cassidy is progressing toward total deafness. His condition is genetic and irreversible, Pres. I'm sorry. There's no magic operation, no miracle cure."

Pres stood up. "I can't accept that." He began to pace. "There must be *some*thing. Some alternative treatment, some recent technological advance—"

"There's nothing," Marsh said gently. "Do you think Molly hasn't searched for some way to preserve her son's hearing?"

"Molly doesn't have the resources or the money—"

"Molly has far more than resources and money. She has her love for her child."

"All the love in the world couldn't help her if there were some million-dollar operation Zander needed—"

"And all the million dollars in the world can't help restore Zander's hearing," Marsh told him. "Pres, I know you don't believe me, but your money can't buy what this little boy needs."

Silence. Pres could hear the sound of his watch as the second hand swept around the dial. "I want to help them," he said again. "Can you give me the names of specialists I can call?"

Marsh gazed at him for a moment, then nodded. "Of course. I'll have Helen fax some names and phone numbers to your office in the morning."

Pres reached across the desk to shake the doctor's hand. "Thanks for seeing me on a Sunday."

Marsh smiled sadly. "I wish it had been for a blood test."

ELEVEN

"SO WE'RE DIVING a wall at about sixty feet," Pres told Zander as they sat on the edge of the pool. "We're right where we're supposed to be, but Simon, this is his first time at this depth, and he's still pretty much a virgin diver, he suddenly panics and instead of taking air *in*to his BC to keep himself neutral, he lets it *out*. Just like that, he goes into free fall, and drops like a stone. I can see him, and I know that he's still panicking, so I go after him. We both go down too far, too fast, about another sixty feet, and I'm not happy about that, but I grab him and adjust his BC and finally get us both neutral again. He's really freaked out, breathing too fast—really sucking the air out of his tank and—"

Pres stopped talking, suddenly aware that Molly was standing beside them. He looked up at her. "Hi."

"And you do this for fun?" she asked, one eyebrow raised.

"Absolutely."

"Did this Simon have fun?"

"Eventually."

"So what'dya do?" Zander asked, eager for the end of the story. "What happened next?"

Molly shifted impatiently. "When you guys are done telling horror stories, *you* need to do your homework," she said, pointing to Zander, "and you . . ." She looked down at Pres. "I'd like to talk to you, if you don't mind."

She turned to go back to the house, but Pres stopped her by reaching out and grasping her ankle. "Hey, how's the work on the roof coming?"

She gently pulled herself free, shading her eyes and looking up at the house. "It's noisy," she admitted, "but hopefully it won't take too much longer. At least not more than a week."

"How about you and me take a walk on the beach," Pres suggested. "Get away from the noise for a while?"

Molly smiled ruefully. "I suppose after three days it's time to give the world another photo opportunity, huh? Lord, I'll be glad after tonight, when this is all over."

"Hey, Mom," Zander said, splashing his feet in the cool water of the pool. "I was thinking.... You know this make-believe game you and Pres are playing, pretending to want to get married and everything, with this big party tonight?"

Molly nodded, waiting for her son to go on, hoping he wasn't going in the direction she feared he was going.

"Well, I was thinking, why don't you just get married for real?"

He went. Straight where she'd hoped he wouldn't go.

Zander turned to look at Pres. "You like us, don't you, Pres? And we like you...."

Molly intercepted, tapping Zander's shoulder so that he would look up at her and correctly follow her words. "Of course Pres likes us, but Z, people just don't go and marry everyone that they like. It's much more serious and complicated than that."

"Why?" Zander asked.

Pres tapped the boy on the leg, and he turned to face him.

"Because when people get married," Pres said, "they should go into that relationship really believing that this is the one person they want to spend the rest of their life with. And the rest of your life can be an awfully long time if you don't pick the right person."

Zander turned his wide blue eyes from Pres to Molly. "And you don't think Mom's the right person?"

Molly closed her eyes. "Zander..."

"Your mom and I don't really know each other that well." Pres glanced up at Molly, a glint of humor in his eyes. "She's pointed that out to me on at least one occasion, and you know, I think she's probably right."

"So you *might* get married, after you know each other," Zander concluded.

"Zander, if I were you, I wouldn't hold my

breath," Molly said. "It's highly unlikely that's going to happen."

"But it's not impossible. Nothing's impossible. You say that all the time." Zander turned back to Pres. "So what happened to Simon?"

Molly mouthed the words *I'm sorry,* to Pres, but he just smiled.

"Okay," he said, getting back to his story. "Simon and I are down at about a hundred and twenty feet, and I know we're in big trouble. We're close to the limit for a no-decompression dive and—remember what I told you about all the time limits for divers because of the water pressure, and how if you dive past a certain depth, you need to take your time coming back to the surface to decompress?"

"Or you'll get the bends," Zander said.

"Right."

Molly backed away. "I'll be up at the house."

"We'll be there in a sec." Pres barely even glanced at her this time, turning back to Zander, who was thoroughly enthralled in the story. "So we're down too deep, and Simon is hyperventilating, which means he's using up his air supply way too quickly and my dive computer is flashing all kinds of warning signals. We've already been down there too long. To be completely honest, Zander, I was more scared than I've ever been before in my entire life."

Molly couldn't help but listen, fascinated and horrified despite herself. She stood quietly by the gate to the pool and watched Pres talk to her son.

"So I make the calculations," Pres told Zander, "and I realize we're in big trouble. Even without Simon breathing too fast, we don't have enough air to get to the surface with all the decompression stops we'll need. And on top of that I can't get Simon calmed down. We're underwater, and I can't talk to him."

"If I learned sign language, and Simon learned sign language, then we could talk under water," Pres signed to Zander. "It would've been easy to calm Simon down if we knew sign language," he said aloud.

Molly had to sit down.

She reached blindly behind her for a lounge chair and sat, staring at Pres in disbelief. How had he managed to learn so much sign language so quickly? Sure, he'd told them that he wanted to learn, but . . .

She'd thought he was just making polite noise, that sign language was one of those things he'd like to learn but would never find the time for. She hadn't believed him. She hadn't thought he was serious.

Obviously he was.

"And when we made our way back to the hundred-foot mark," Pres was telling Zander, "there was the rest of our dive team, waiting for us with spare tanks. Thanks to them, we made it to the surface, took our time, had plenty of air, and nobody got bent."

"Cool," Zander said, awe in his voice.

"You know what the moral of that story is?" Pres asked.

Zander shook his head.

"Never, *ever* dive alone, and if possible, dive in teams of more than two."

Zander nodded reverently, as if Pres had just imparted some incredible gem of wisdom.

Pres smiled at Zander. "I think it's homework time now."

Zander glanced quickly back at Molly. "Yeah. I guess."

"Do you have a lot?"

Another glance at Molly. "I don't know. Not too much."

"Will you be okay, hanging out here while Molly and I go for a walk?"

Zander nodded. "Sure." He started to dash past Molly, but skidded to a stop. "Mom, can I have a snack?"

"Yes." He was gone before the word was out of her mouth.

Pres unwrapped a piece of chewing gum and folded it into his mouth as he approached Molly at a much slower pace. She stood up, still incredulous.

"I can't believe you're really learning to sign. When? *How?* I'm speechless."

Pres smiled. "You can't be speechless..." he said, then signed, "...if you know sign language."

His hands were graceful, his fingers long and really quite beautiful. Somehow they managed to be both elegant *and* work-roughened—just like the man himself.

"Considering that you've been avoiding me since Saturday night, and I've had a whole lot of free time, I took advantage of the opportunity and got some books about signing. And Zander's been teaching me too."

"I haven't been avoiding you," Molly protested. "At least, not *exactly* . . ."

"Let's walk." He took her hand with an easy familiarity, and together they started down the path that led to the beach. He glanced over his shoulder at her. "What's on your agenda? I got the sense that this was going to be a talk with a capital *T.*"

"About tonight . . ."

"Can't avoid me tonight, Molly. There's no way you can cancel. We've got a guest list of over five hundred people."

"Five *hundred*?"

"Roughly."

"I'm not going to cancel. I'm just . . . nervous."

As they reached the open sand of the beach, Pres slipped his arm around her shoulders so that they were walking arm in arm. "I'll be there, right next to you the entire time."

"*That's* what's making me nervous."

She fit perfectly against him. Whether they were dancing or walking or even kissing, they were a near-perfect match. She tried to put some space between them, but he wouldn't let her go.

"Uh-oh, photographers, dead ahead," he murmured. He tugged Molly toward him, covering her mouth with his in a lingering kiss.

His mouth was as sweet as she remembered. And she *did* remember. Vividly. In fact, she'd been dreaming about his kisses now for three nights running. Kisses, and more.

"That's why I've been avoiding you," she admonished him breathlessly.

"Aha, so you admit it. You *have* been avoiding me."

She turned to face him. "You want the truth?"

For a fraction of a second Pres considered saying no. No, he didn't want to know the truth. He had a feeling that it wasn't going to be something he wanted to hear. But he nodded. "Yes. Please. Tell me the truth."

"I like you too much," she told him bluntly. "I'm afraid I'm going to do something really stupid, like sleep with you."

This wasn't a bad truth. This was a good truth. A very, *very* good truth. "Would that be so terrible?"

Molly looked down at her bare feet as she scratched a line into the sand with one toe. She didn't need to answer, he could see it on her face. Yes, it would be terrible.

But she was wrong, and he was determined to convince her otherwise.

Pres reached for her hand and they began to walk again, the photographers slowly trailing along about fifty yards behind them, just far enough away to give them the illusion of privacy.

Molly glanced up at him. "I almost called you back yesterday."

"I wish you had."

She squinted slightly as she gazed out over the sparkling blue ocean. The wind swept her hair into her face, and she used her other hand to brush it out of her eyes. "Zander and I went to the library, and while we were there the librarian told us that the most wonderful thing has happened—an anonymous donor gave a present to the library in the form of five thousand compact discs—along with shelves to store them."

Pres didn't even try to deny that he was the mysterious donor. "You told me you didn't want me to give Zander such a big gift, so I did the next best thing. I gave it to the public library. This way, he has access to a huge collection of music, and I haven't overstepped your boundaries."

"You're amazing," Molly said, but the tone of her voice wasn't quite admiration. "You don't take no for an answer, do you? When someone tells you no, you don't give up. You find another solution and somehow manage to get your way."

"You say that as if that's something bad."

Molly stopped walking, turning toward him. "It's not—at least not in this case. Giving the library an extensive CD collection was a wonderful idea. I know how expensive it must've been, and I thank you for that. But..." She took a deep breath. "I find myself wondering about the other things I've said no to. You wanted to buy the Kirk Estate and I said no. You invited me back to your room and I said no. I can't help but think that sooner or later, despite my saying no, you're going to get what you want."

God, he hoped so. But he didn't dare say those words aloud. He glanced over his shoulder at the photographers and they started walking again, but Molly persisted.

"I got a very interesting phone call today," she

continued. "From someone named Simon Hunt, from the Sunrise Key Historical Society—which, incidentally and quite oddly, didn't seem to exist before just a few days ago."

Pres knew what was coming.

"Simon Hunt," she repeated, looking up at him. "That wouldn't be the same Simon from the scuba-diving story you were telling Zander, would it?"

"It would."

"Of course. I'm happy to hear he's survived until now. Anyway, Mr. Hunt informed me that the Kirk Estate has been awarded a restoration grant to the tune of one hundred thousand dollars."

"Congratulations."

"As if you didn't know about it," Molly accused him. "As if you weren't the sole financial backer behind this so-called Sunrise Key Historical Society."

"If you're going to restore the Kirk Estate, you should do it right."

"Which means doing it *your* way," she countered. "Right?"

"I happen to believe that restoration involves

reusing as much of the original materials as possible and—"

"I was sent a copy of the grant," Molly said. "The fine print said that any restoration done on the house would need to be approved by a liaison from the historical society. Gee, I wonder who that will turn out to be?"

"It'll be me."

"Big surprise. The grant also mentioned a teeny little detail about the resale of the house. According to the agreement, if I accept the grant money, I have to give the Sunrise Key Historical Society *and its benefactor* the right of first refusal if I ever decide to sell." She gazed steadily at him. "Look me in the eye and tell me that you're not the benefactor."

Pres looked her in the eye. "You're absolutely right. I'm the benefactor."

"And according to this grant, I'll need to get your approval even if I want to replace something as trivial as the grout around a loose tile in the bathroom...?" Her voice rang with disbelief.

"Believe it or not, there are different types of grout that were used depending on—"

"Dear Lord, I *knew* it! If I accept this grant, I'll

end up restoring this entire house with *your* money, *your* way. With *you* breathing down my neck the entire time." Molly pulled her hand away from his and began walking rapidly back toward the house.

Pres caught up with her easily. "Would that really be so terrible? Working closely with me that way?"

Molly spun to face him, and he nearly tripped over her. "Maybe you could clear up one thing that I'm not certain of here," she said, spitting fire. "Are you using the house to try to sleep with me, or are you trying to sleep with me to get ahold of the house?"

Pres couldn't help it. He had to laugh, and unfortunately, that only made her more furious. He caught her arm before she could run away again, and got real serious, real fast.

"Molly, come on. Wait. I don't even *want* your house anymore." As he spoke the words he realized that they were the truth. He didn't want the Kirk Estate.

Molly glanced toward the photographers and lowered her voice. "And you expect me just to believe you."

"Yeah," he said. "I don't want to buy your house, because I want you and Zander to stay here on Sunrise Key."

Molly stared at Pres. Her burst of anger was fading fast, leaving behind a swirl of other emotions. They were strange emotions that mixed peculiarly with the remnants of the anger—something that felt remarkably like pleasure and this odd fluttering sensation of anticipation in her stomach.

"If I buy your house," he continued, "then you'll leave. And I don't want you to leave."

She couldn't believe what she was hearing. "But the grant..."

"Right of first refusal is pretty much standard boilerplate in this kind of private funding," Pres told her. "At least that's what my lawyer told me."

"So you're just giving me a hundred thousand dollars...?"

"It's tax-deductible."

"Oh, *that* explains it."

Molly couldn't handle this—not what she was hearing and especially not what she was feeling. She went down to the water and stood with the gentle Gulf waves lapping over her feet. Pres followed, as she knew he would, but she couldn't look at him. She didn't want to look at him, didn't want to feel her insides start to melt when he flashed her one of his killer smiles. She didn't want to feel the quickening of anticipation when he brushed against her. She didn't want her heart to race when she gazed into his eyes.

"What exactly do you want from me, Pres?" she asked. She wasn't brave enough to turn her head and meet his gaze.

Pres didn't answer right away. It should have been a simple question. He wanted her. He wanted to make love to her. He wanted her to be his lover.

He wanted a cigarette. He forcefully pushed that thought away.

Yes, he wanted to be Molly's lover, but he also wanted more. He'd known for days, when every time he called she made some excuse not to see him. He'd known when every time he'd dropped by, she'd asked him to stay with Zander for a few hours while she ran some errands. He'd known the truth. This was about more than mere sex.

He wanted to be with Molly, to talk with her,

to make her laugh, to watch her smile. He wanted to share more with her than passion in bed. He wanted to share her joy and love for Zander, and even her pain of knowing her son's deafness was worsening little by little, day by day. He wanted to share her life, to commingle it with his life, so neither of them would ever be alone again. He wanted a family. He wanted that ring he'd put on Molly's finger to be real.

He wanted too much, too soon.

Too much, too soon—that described his short affair and rushed marriage with Merrilee Fender. That had been a total disaster. There was no way he was going to make that same mistake again.

That was why he hadn't pushed when over the past few days Molly had repeatedly turned down his dinner invitations. Although hot and heavy best described his impulsive style when it came to both his personal and business life, Pres was trying his hardest to follow Molly's lead and take whatever this was they shared between them extremely slowly.

After all, he'd been wrong before.

What did he want from her? she'd asked. He brought it all down to the simplest equation.

"You know what I want. I want to see where this thing between us can go."

She nodded slowly, still looking out at the ocean, where the gleaming white sails of a boat moved slowly across the horizon. "You know damn well that the first place it would go is right into your bed."

"I can't deny that I want to make love to you," he said evenly. "You know that I do."

"So this is about sex," Molly said. "And the hundred-thousand-dollar grant is supposed to be some kind of billionaire-style foreplay?"

Pres couldn't help but laugh. "No."

"Then is it some kind of payment?"

He turned her to face him. "Of course not. One thing has absolutely nothing to do with the other."

"I find that hard to believe—combined with the huge gift you gave to the library." Molly met his eyes squarely. "Not to mention that amazingly expensive dress and shoes you sent to the house for me to wear to the party tonight. And I stopped in at Dr. Devlin's office this morning to pick up some forms for the school, and he told me you'd been by, asking all kinds of questions about degenerative hearing loss. You went to see the doctor because you thought maybe there was some ultraexpensive operation you could buy to make Zander all better, right?"

Pres couldn't deny it. "Yes, but—"

"I wish there were," Molly said. "But God help me, if there were, I would have already found a way for Zander to have that operation, regardless of the cost. Money isn't the solution to every problem, Pres. Believe it or not, there are some things money can't buy."

"I know that—"

"And I'm one of them. I'm not going to accept the historical society's grant."

She started walking up the beach, toward the path to the house. Frustrated, Pres followed, well aware of the small crowd of photographers and news cameras trailing after them.

"Molly, I'm not trying to buy you."

She stopped walking, glancing quickly toward the cameras before looking up into his eyes. "Are you sure?" she asked quietly.

Then she put her arms around him and gave him the gentlest and sweetest of kisses, all for the benefit of those cameras.

"Don't follow me back to the house," she told him. "And smile. Zander and I will see you tonight."

Pres caught her hand. "I'm *not* trying to buy you."

She smiled for the cameras as she pulled free, then hurried up the hot sand toward the shaded path.

She didn't say the words again, but they seemed to echo in Pres's head as he watched her go.

Are you sure?

TWELVE

PRES KNOCKED TWICE on the door of the suite next to his. An hour ago he'd sent Lenny, his driver, over to pick up Molly and Zander and bring them to the resort. He'd thought it might be easier for them to get dressed for the party away from the dust and rubble of the Kirk Estate's restorations, and Molly had agreed.

Pres knocked again, louder this time, and Zander opened the door.

The boy was wearing a white dress shirt tucked haphazardly into a pair of tan dress pants. Attached to his collar was a crooked clip-on tie. As usual, his glasses were slightly askew and his hair stood straight up in several places.

"Mom's still in the bedroom, getting dressed." He gazed at Pres, stepping back to let him into the suite. "You look ... funny."

"Gee, thanks, Z."

"I don't mean funny ha-ha," Zander explained. "I mean funny weird."

"That's better?" Pres glanced in the entryway mirror and adjusted his tuxedo jacket.

Zander looked at himself in the mirror, too, and futilely tried to comb down his hair. "You look like you come from one of those old movies Mom loves."

That *was* better. "You want me to help you with that?" Pres offered.

Zander handed him the comb. "I have problem hair."

"You need to wet it down," Pres suggested, trying hard not to smile. One of the bedroom doors was closed, so he led Zander toward the other one. The boy followed him into the bathroom that was attached and stood patiently as Pres wet the comb under the faucet.

"Did you get all your homework done?" Pres asked as he combed Zander's hair.

Zander chewed on his lower lip. "Sort of."

"Sort of? How can you sort of do your homework? Either you do it or you don't."

Zander met Pres's gaze in the mirror, then quickly looked away. "I sort of . . . don't have any homework."

Pres set the comb down on the sink counter, watching the boy in the mirror. "I thought fifth graders had homework most schoolnights."

"They do."

"I see. But you don't."

"No."

Silence. It stretched on and on and on.

Pres finally asked, "You want to tell me what's going on?"

Zander hesitated. "School isn't going too well," he finally admitted. "The kids are nice—they're great in fact—but my teacher, Mr. Towne . . ."

Pres felt his heart sink. Of course. Stanley Towne was Zander's teacher. He'd heard the man's name many times before, and never connected to anything complimentary. As far as Pres could figure it, Towne had burned out as a teacher years ago. He was unpleasant and grouchy and generally disliked. But because of his tenure in the school system, he couldn't be let go.

"When Mr. Towne writes on the blackboard," Zander told Pres, "he turns his back, and he keeps talking, but I can't read his lips, so I don't know what he's saying. He also talks to the class while he's sitting on the shelf in front of the windows, and because of the glare, I can't see his lips then, either. Sometimes he walks around the room, and..." Zander shook his head, his face pinched and anxious. The words came out faster now, a steady stream of information. "He talks so softly and smooshes all his words together with his funny accent. Most of the time I don't know what's going on. The first day, I didn't even *know* we had a homework assignment. But then yesterday, everyone handed something in—except for me. I tried to explain to Mr. Towne. I tried to tell him that I couldn't hear him or read his lips the way he moved around the room, and he told me he had no training in special education and he's not going to change his habits now. He told me I shouldn't even be in his class, so I shouldn't bother to do the homework." Zander swallowed. "He told me he doesn't believe in special-education kids coming into a regular classroom, and he wants to have me sent to a school for the deaf that's over on the mainland."

Pres was outraged. "He said all that? To you?"

Zander nodded, tears in his eyes.

"Turn off your hearing aids, Zander, I'm about to use some language your mom probably wouldn't want you to hear."

Zander smiled crookedly, wiping his eyes. "I know all those words. I even know American Sign Language for some of them."

"I know one international sign that I'd like to give Stan Towne," Pres said. "In fact, I ought to take my diving spear and pay him a visit."

Zander giggled, his tears all but forgotten. "Mom would have a cow."

"Speaking of your mom," Pres added. "I'm assuming you haven't mentioned any of this to her."

The boy's wide blue eyes got even wider as he shook his head. "Are you kidding? She'd be so mad, she'd want to punch Mr. Towne in the nose!"

"She'd have to stand in line," Pres muttered.

"You've got to tell your mom what you told me," he added, louder.

"But what if she wants to go back to New York? I had a really great teacher in New York, but I don't want to go back there. I like it better here, even if Mr. Towne stinks."

"Still, you have to tell her."

"Maybe he'll get better."

"Do you really think that?"

"Maybe. Or maybe he'll go away and we'll get a new teacher. Nothing's impossible," Zander insisted.

Maybe, just maybe Mr. Towne *would* go away. "You're right," Pres agreed. "Nothing's impossible."

"Ms. Cassidy, do you have a comment regarding the rumors of Mr. Seaholm's breakup with his first wife, Merrilee Fender, being due to his sexual dysfunction?"

"I most certainly do have a comment," Molly said crisply and quite sternly, unable to turn her head and meet Pres's gaze, "and my comment is to ask you, sir, where you get the audacity to ask such a personal question in the first place?"

"So in other words, no comment?" the reporter persisted.

"Saying 'no comment' is fine," Pres breathed in her ear, his arm tightening around her waist.

"For your information, the rumors are absolutely and completely untrue." She felt Pres kiss her lightly, just beside her ear.

"Thanks," he murmured.

Thank God Zander had already left the party, returning to their hotel suite with Pres's friend Dominic as babysitter. She could just imagine the questions Zander would ask, and her attempts to define such things as sexual dysfunction.

"Ms. Cassidy, what does it feel like to be engaged to marry one of the richest men in America?"

This question was one she could answer more easily. "Don't you mean one of the richest, most handsome, and nicest men in America?" she countered. "Do you guys need help spelling the word *nice*? N-I-C-E. You probably don't have much cause to use that word in your line of work...."

Pres was looking at her with a smile dancing in his hazel eyes. Molly found herself smiling back at him—after all, who wouldn't? Dressed in that figure-hugging tuxedo, he was quite possibly the best-looking man alive. His shoulders were impossibly broad, his waist and hips trim. For a guy who spent most of his time in Bermuda shorts and faded T-shirts, he wore his tux with an easy confidence and cool authority.

"Actually," Molly said, still gazing into Preston's eyes, "it feels an awful lot like a fairy tale. Here I am at the ball with Prince Delectable—the luckiest one of the hundred and one princesses who have been imported into his kingdom, hoping to catch his royal eye." She turned to look out at the reporters. "Do you know the story of Prince Delectable? He held the title of most eligible bachelor in his kingdom too."

"I don't know that story," Pres murmured.

"Zander has it in one of his books," she told him.

"Mr. Seaholm! Is it true you're planning to teach Molly's ten-year-old son to skydive?"

"Skydive? No." Pres reluctantly pulled his gaze away from Molly's, leaning forward slightly to speak into the microphones. "I will start teaching the boy how to snorkel, though."

Pres sensed more than felt Molly stiffen alongside him. Damn, he shouldn't have brought this up. "With his mother's permission, of course," he quickly added.

"Mr. Seaholm, have you and Ms. Cassidy set a wedding date?"

"Not yet, no," Pres told the reporter. "Now, if you'll excuse us, I want to dance with my bride-to-be."

The cameras and photographers followed them up to the outdoor deck where the dance band was playing. The dance floor was only sparsely filled, and Pres gently pulled Molly into his arms.

"At dinner the other night I felt as if I were in a goldfish bowl," Molly remarked. "Tonight I feel like I'm in a zoo. Not just any zoo, but one of those really sleazy kinds, where you pay extra to go into the tent to see the two-headed calf."

Pres laughed. "You're much better looking than a two-headed calf." He pulled her closer. "Have I told you how great you look tonight?"

Molly was wearing the dress he'd bought for her. It was a shimmering and ethereal white with a rather modest, high neckline and a low-scooped back. She wore her hair down, and it gleamed around her shoulders. She looked a mystifying combination of angel and girl next door.

"Only five thousand times."

"So did this Prince Delectable and his princess live happily ever after?"

"Actually," Molly said, "the prince ended up with someone else entirely."

"Who?" Pres pulled her close enough so that his cheek brushed the soft silk of her hair.

"He discovered that early on, before the story even starts, he'd already given his heart to the girl who lives next door."

Pres had to smile. The girl next door...

"We haven't had a moment to ourselves all evening." He danced Molly away from the cameras, into a shadowy and more secluded corner of the deck.

"Maybe that's good."

"No, it's not good, because I wanted to talk to you," he told her. "I've been thinking about what you said—about trying to buy your affection." He paused, looking down at her, gathering strength from the calm blueness of her eyes.

"Maybe you were a little bit right. Maybe part of me was testing you—to see if you *could* be bought." He shook his head, smiling ruefully. "I don't know, it's kind of complicated. A part of me wants you badly enough to pay any price to have you. And there's this other part that's hoping you'll keep turning my money down."

Molly was holding her breath, aware that she and Pres were entering uncharted territory. He was telling her how he felt. He was sharing a tiny piece of himself with her.

"Can we take a walk on the beach?" he asked, tugging her gently toward the stairs that led down from the deck onto the soft moonlit sand. "I want to tell you about something that happened to me. Maybe then you'll understand."

Intrigued, Molly followed, stopping at the last step to slip off her shoes and leave them next to Preston's along a low concrete seawall. She slipped the narrow strap of her tiny purse over her shoulder and together they stepped barefoot into the cool sand.

Music drifted hauntingly down onto the beach, and Pres took her in his arms, spinning her around on the sand. The moon was nearly full and the ocean seemed to glisten, murmuring softly as the tide continued its rush inward.

They walked down the beach for a while in silence, leaving the lights from the main resort building behind them.

Finally, Pres began to speak. "About two and a half years ago," he told her, pulling her forward so that the cool water lapped over their bare toes, "I met Merrilee Fender."

Molly didn't say a word. She just listened, waiting for him to go on.

"She was working here at the resort at the time, as part of the cleaning staff. I noticed her almost right away...." He gave Molly a rueful glance and a somewhat sheepish shrug. "It would have been hard not to—she was strikingly attractive. But we didn't meet at the resort. I ran into her downtown, at the dive shop. She was posting a notice on the bulletin board—looking for a dive buddy. It seemed kind of like fate."

He took a deep breath and let it slowly out. "She was perfect. She was everything I thought I wanted in a woman. Tall, blond, elegant, poised, not too clingy, but not overly independent, either. She was a certified scuba diver and she knew how to windsurf. She knew about investments and the stock market. She could cook Italian food—my favorite—like you wouldn't believe. We'd read all the same books, loved all the same movies. . . . I fell for her hard and fast. Every time I turned around, she was even more perfect. So after this incredible, whirlwind, two-week romance, I married her."

The moonlight created shadows across his face as he looked down at her and tried to smile.

"So what went wrong?" she asked softly, trying hard not to feel jealous of perfect Merrilee Fender. Clearly he'd loved the woman. And it was possible, despite his denial, that he loved her still. And why shouldn't he? Merrilee *was* perfect.

"Everything," he said flatly. "Three weeks after the wedding Merrilee started talking about a movie that was being cast over in Orlando. I knew the producers quite well—we'd done business together a few years back. Merri told me she'd always loved to 'dabble in theater'—I think that was the way she put it. She asked me to call the producers and get her a screen test.

"She really wanted to do it, so I figured what the hell, and I made the call. Her screen test was good, but nothing out of the ordinary. But Merrilee told me that the producers were looking for some outside money, and if I invested, she'd get the part. And she really, really wanted the part. So I invested. And she was cast. And she was sensational. And the offers for other roles started coming in.

"She was excited, but I wasn't. We'd just spent three months in Orlando while she made this movie, and now she wanted to pack up and go out to Hollywood without even taking a break. She had all these contracts lined up, one right after the other for the next two and a half years and ..." He shook his head. "I told her we were going to have to compromise. I needed to spend at least half the year on Sunrise Key, at the resort. I really wanted to be there more often. I love Sunrise Key, it's my home, but I figured I was married now, and to make it work, I'd have to give some of that up. But she looked me in the eye and told me that six months wasn't enough. She told me that she wanted a divorce.

"I was blown away. I didn't see it coming, didn't have a clue. It was crazy—we'd only been married four months."

"But you gave her the divorce," Molly said.

"Yeah. I wanted to go into counseling, to see if we could work this out." He paused, gazing up at the moon as if it held all of the answers. "Until she told me the truth."

"The truth?" Molly echoed softly.

"I've never told anyone this before," he said, turning to look at her. His eyes looked crystal and colorless in the pale light, and shockingly intense. "But I was conned, Molly. Right from the start. Merrilee came after me because of my friendship with these movie producers and my money. She *researched* me, and became this perfect woman— perfect for me. She learned to dive and windsurf, she read all my favorite books, learned to cook my favorite food. . . . She was acting. It was all one big, incredible, Academy Award–winning act. None of it was real. After she told me the truth, I gave her the divorce. I also made her sign off on all requests for alimony, all financial settlements. Not that she complained. She got what she wanted—the screen test and that initial invest-ment that bought her the part."

"You must've been very badly hurt," Molly said quietly.

"I was devastated." He forced another smile. "I never told anyone *that* before either."

"I know I asked you this already, but . . . do you still love her?" Molly held her breath, afraid to find out the answer, but needing to know.

"She wasn't real." Pres looked out over the silvery ocean. "I was in love with a fictional character. The person I thought I loved didn't really exist. Even her name was fake, can you believe that? Her real name was Rachel. She changed it because she thought I'd like Merrilee better." He shook his head. "When I found out it was all a lie, it was as if someone I loved had died."

He looked into her eyes. "So, no. I don't still love her. The woman I thought I loved wasn't real."

Molly nodded. "Look on the bright side—after a while you would've gotten bored with all that endless perfection."

Pres smiled—his first genuine smile since he'd started telling her this story. "So now do you understand why I would never want to buy someone's love? And why I might try it, just to see what it really is that they want from me?"

"I don't want your money, Pres. And I have no desire to be a movie star. I want . . ."

"Tell me. You know what I want. Tell me what *you* want."

Molly felt dizzy, lost in the bottomless depths of his eyes. "I want you to kiss me."

He gazed at her for a moment, and then he smiled. It was that same hot, fierce smile he'd first given to her up on the roof of her house with thunder crashing around them. She'd seen that smile half a dozen times since, and it always took her breath away. It was a reflection of the passion and the excitement and the pure, heartfelt joy of life that was so much a part of this man.

And then he kissed her. Most of his other kisses before this had been careful and controlled, Molly realized as he nearly lifted her off her feet. But this was like that first kiss they'd shared in her living room. This was hot and urgent and deliriously, deliciously wild. His tongue invaded her mouth as he crushed her against him, and still she wanted more. She wanted deeper kisses. She wanted to be even closer to him.

His thigh parted her legs and she heard herself moan.

"Molly, my bungalow is right over on the other side of those trees," he whispered as he kissed her eyelids, her cheeks, her throat. "God, I want to make love to you...."

His bungalow. Not his suite. His bungalow. The home into which he never let anyone else enter. Tonight he'd shared with her the story of his unhappy marriage to Merrilee Fender. And now he was going to share himself with her again, by bringing her into his most personal and private space.

She couldn't say no. She didn't want to say no.

So she said yes.

THIRTEEN

PRES UNLOCKED the door to his bungalow, nervous as hell, and desperate for a cigarette. He knew where he still had some. There was an unopened pack in the far left drawer in the kitchen. He hadn't been able to bring himself to throw it away.

Molly was nervous too. He watched her as he shut the door behind her and turned the overhead ceiling fan on low to circulate the air-conditioned air. She looked around at the tiny living room.

"This is nice." She turned to glance back at

him. "I thought you said your furniture doesn't match."

"It doesn't," he said. "Not the way the stuff up at the resort matches."

She looked at the paintings that hung on the wall, stopping in front of one of his favorites. She leaned closer, squinting at the signature and date, then turned to look back at him in astonishment. "Is this . . . ?"

Pres nodded, shrugging out of his tuxedo jacket. "Yeah. It's mine. I'm pretty good at water and sky. But as soon as I try adding boats or people or birds, it all gets messed up."

"Do you paint every day?"

"As long as it's not raining. It's rained an awful lot this spring." He went into the attached kitchen. "Can I get you something to drink?"

Molly followed him, taking her tiny bag off her shoulder and setting it down on the counter. "Is this weird or what? I mean, here we are, making nice, polite conversation. But it's not as if we didn't come here for a reason. . . ."

He had to smile. "I thought I'd follow some social conventions and offer you a drink before tearing off your clothes."

She smiled back at him. "How gentlemanly of you. But it still feels weird. I mean, can we talk about something a little bit deeper than the weather?"

Pres took two glasses down from the cabinet. "I'm afraid it's a choice between lemonade, seltzer, or beer."

Molly laughed. "Oh, that's *much* deeper than the weather."

"I didn't get to the deep part yet," he protested.

"Do you have ice?" she asked.

"Of course."

"Fill the glasses with ice and pour half a bottle of beer into each glass," she instructed.

"Beer over ice? Are you kidding?"

"Do you trust me?"

Time stood completely still for a moment as Pres gazed into her eyes. Molly had come here to make love to him. He knew that and she knew that. It was only a matter of time before he took her hand and led her back into his bedroom and . . . He moistened his suddenly dry lips. "Yes. I trust you completely."

She smiled. "Then do it."

He did.

"Now fill the rest of the glass with seltzer, and a splash of lemonade."

"Just tell me honestly, is this going to taste as awful as I think it's going to taste?"

"It's going to taste remarkably refreshing," she told him, watching as he followed her instructions.

Pres handed one of the glasses to Molly. He took a sip.

"What do you think?" she asked.

It *was* remarkably refreshing, the beer flavor mixing curiously with the tart lemon. "I think that it's been two years since I built this bungalow," he said, "and you're the first person I've even invited inside." He took another sip of his drink, watching her over the rim of his glass. "That deep enough for you?"

Molly nodded. "I figure you're either really, *really* horny, or maybe you actually like me," she said dryly.

He laughed. "Actually, I really, *really* like you." He didn't dare use the word he really meant.

"I like you too," she admitted. Her voice got softer. "I like it when you talk to me. I like that you brought me here—that you'd share your secrets with me. I know that talking about Merrilee couldn't have been easy."

"It wasn't, but it was," Pres said. "I don't know, Molly, but when I'm with you, everything's easy."

She put her drink down on the counter. "Tell me another secret."

He put his drink down too. "I was thinking that maybe it's time to get to the tearing-off-your-clothes part of this seduction."

Molly laughed, backing away from him. "That's no secret. Tell me... tell me what your dreams are."

Pres stopped short. "Nobody's ever asked me that before," he mused.

"Really?"

"I think everyone assumes that because of my money, I'm living my dreams," he told her. "In some ways I am, but..."

"So what are they?"

He glanced away from her. "I don't know...."

"You want to scuba-dive around the world," she guessed. "You want to skydive out of the space shuttle. You want to be the first billionaire on the moon—"

"No, believe it or not, it's nothing like that. In fact, it's pretty damn hokey. . . ."

"Hokier than being the first billionaire on the moon?" Molly asked with mock amazement.

"Now I'm not going to tell you."

"You know, it's a real turn-on for me when you tell me personal things about yourself."

He laughed. "Yeah, right." But still he looked at her closely to see if just maybe she was telling the truth.

She had to smile at that look in his eyes. It was probably just as good that he thought she was only teasing. "Why don't you tell me your hokey dream and watch me melt?"

He moved closer. "I think I need a kiss to give me strength."

Molly could feel her heart pounding as he touched her—first lightly on the shoulders, and then gently cupping her face. He was going to kiss her. They were alone, in the privacy of his home, and he was going to kiss her. The blinds were all down, the curtains drawn, and he was going to kiss her. Kiss her and more. Much more.

He smiled into her eyes as he lowered his

mouth to hers and then, Lord, she was kissing him.

It was a gentle kiss, different from that kiss on the beach. He was holding back, taking his time, as if he were afraid he'd scare her off if he let himself go.

It was as if he wanted to make sure she was here with him because she wanted to be—not because she was swept up in the moment. It was as if he wanted to make sure she knew she could still change her mind and walk away.

She knew it was crazy. She'd probably live to regret it. But she wasn't going anywhere.

Molly laced her fingers through the hair at the nape of his neck and he closed his eyes, sighing his pleasure. He pulled her closer, his hands sweeping down the open back of her dress, his work-callused fingers slightly rough against her skin. The sensation was exquisite.

He kissed her again, less carefully now, and she could feel the unmistakable evidence of his desire. He wanted her. He wanted *her*.

And she wanted him. Desperately. Frantically.

It was such a relief to finally admit it, such a relief to finally give in.

Molly pulled away from him, breathless. "If this is some kind of attempt to distract me so you won't have to tell me about this dream of yours—it's working."

Pres laughed, but the heat in his eyes didn't fade. "Right now I only have one dream—and I think it's about to come true."

"You only *think* so? I *know* so." Molly reached up and untied his bow tie. Holding both ends, she began leading him toward his bedroom.

Preston's pulse kicked into double time. "Hey, who's in charge of this seduction here?"

She started unbuttoning his shirt. "Looks to me as if I'm seducing you."

He laughed. "Lady, you had me thoroughly seduced five minutes after we met."

Molly pushed his tuxedo shirt off his tanned shoulders and smiled sweetly up at him. "In that case, you must be seducing me." She kissed his neck as she ran her hands lightly up and down the smooth muscles of his chest. "You're doing an excellent job, but..."

"But?"

"Remember how I wanted you to take things nice and slow...don't move too fast, keep everything under control?"

Her featherlight touch was almost too much to bear, yet Pres didn't want her to stop.

"Yeah." His own voice sounded choked, tight. "I've been trying...."

"I've changed my mind."

Pres didn't need to hear her say it twice. He kissed her hard as he shook his arms free from his shirtsleeves. His hands swept down the curve of her derriere, pulling her hips in tightly to him, and she opened herself to him, pressing up against his thigh. He could feel her heat, taste her need as he kissed her even harder, deeper, longer. He slid his hand between them and held a little piece of heaven as he cupped the soft fullness of her breast. She moaned as his thumb found the hard bud of her nipple and he breathed his own pleasure in unison with hers.

Dear God, he'd never wanted anyone as much as he wanted this woman. He was dizzy with desire, delirious from the knowledge that she belonged to him. At least for tonight.

But tonight wasn't going to be enough. He

wanted more. He wanted...Mother of God, he wanted forever. He wanted to tell Molly that he loved her, that if she'd let him, he would love her until the end of time.

But he wasn't sure that she was going to let him.

He wasn't even sure he'd be telling her the truth.

Too much, too soon. He'd felt this euphoria with Merrilee. He'd fallen hard and fast with his ex-wife, too, and look where *that* had gotten him.

But decisions about forever could be put off until the future. Tonight, however, there was no need to hesitate.

Pres swept Molly up into his arms and carried her into his bedroom. He could feel her hands unfastening his pants, and then, *God,* she was touching him.

She laughed at his explosive cry of pleasure, and pulled him down so they tumbled together onto his bed. Her hair was in his face as she kissed him, touched him, stroked him, drove him totally insane. He fumbled for the zipper on the back of her dress, distracted by his need to touch the softness of her breasts, the smoothness of her thighs, the utter sweetness of her.

"Do you have protection?" she asked as she struggled to sit up. She pushed his pants down his legs.

Protection? He didn't know. He didn't even know his name. All he knew was that he wanted her surrounding him, and he wanted her now. He reached for her dress and pulled it up and over her head.

Her underwear was white and made of lace and her skin was smooth and pale. She didn't have a tan. Somehow that fact registered, and he realized hazily that he'd never seen her on the beach. Of course not. She was always working, cleaning up the Kirk Estate, taking care of Zander. She didn't have time for the beach.

Her skin felt so soft as he entangled their legs, and his senses went into overload. He kissed her hard, harder, touching the excruciating silkiness of her skin, aching to bury himself inside of her.

She pulled him on top of her, opening her legs to him, and he went eagerly, straining against the lace barrier that kept them both from total ecstasy. He took one of her rose-colored nipples into his mouth, sucking and pulling right through the lace of her bra and she cried out, her legs tightening around him.

He reached for the front clasp of her bra, but she beat him to it, opening it for him, giving herself to him. He buried his face in the softness of her breasts, inhaling her sweetness, loving her completely, body and soul.

"Pres . . ." Molly tried to push her panties off, but he was on top of her.

Protection. She'd asked him about protection. He wanted in, and she wanted him there, and not for the first time that evening Pres considered breaking his safe-sex rule. Just once. He'd ease himself inside of her and . . . And once wouldn't be enough. He'd never be able to stop, and then, God, she'd get pregnant and then she'd *have* to marry him, and he'd spend the rest of his life in a relationship based on obligation, not love.

And he wanted her to love him. He wanted their babies to be made intentionally, on purpose. He wanted to look into her eyes and smile as he drove his seed deep inside of her, knowing that the miracle of their love was, right at that moment, creating the equally awesome miracle of a precious new life.

No, right now those sexy lace panties were the only thing keeping them both from making an enormous mistake. Because what was he doing fantasizing about making babies with a woman he barely knew?

But when he kissed her, she tasted so deliciously familiar. When he held her in his arms, she fit so perfectly.

Pres kissed her, and then he kissed her again. "I've got a condom in my wallet," he somehow managed to tell her. "Let me get it."

"Hurry," she whispered.

Pres hurried. He found the leg of his pants turned inside out, dangling over the side of the bed. His wallet was still in the back pocket and he quickly opened it and . . .

It wasn't there.

He searched through again and again.

It still wasn't there.

It didn't make sense. He *always* carried a condom in his wallet, and it had been at *least* a year since he'd used the last one and . . .

He'd taken the old one out. He'd taken it out,

intending to replace it with a fresh new one, in hopes of something happening with Molly very much like what was happening right now.

Only he'd forgotten to put the new one back in.

"I don't have a condom." He said the words aloud, and then had to laugh at the sheer ridiculousness of them. Here he was, mere moments from getting what he'd been dying for, and he didn't have any protection. It was too absurd.

Molly propped herself up on her elbows, and he turned to look at her.

"I didn't put one in my wallet," he said. "And I don't keep any in the house."

"You don't?"

God, she looked sexy, lying back like that on his bed. Her hair was rumpled and her legs were slightly spread and...

Pres laughed. He had to laugh, or he was going to start to cry. "Of course I don't keep any here. I've never invited anyone over before and they're not the kind of thing you have much use for when you're alone." He took a deep breath, letting it out hard and fast. "Okay," he said, more to himself than to Molly. "Okay. This isn't the end of the world. There's always tomorrow, right?" He crawled back toward her and pulled her into his arms, kissing her. "And tonight I can still give you pleasure...."

Molly pulled back. "You've really never brought a woman here before, have you?"

"I really haven't." He trailed kisses down her neck and lower, stopping to touch each of her nipples with the very tip of his tongue. His hands swept even lower, parting her legs. She was slick and hot with her desire for him.

Pres closed his eyes, willing the intense wave of his own wants and needs to pass. He burned for her, throbbed for her, ached for her. But that was going to have to wait, because when it came to Molly, he was damned if he was going to make a mistake.

She shivered at his touch, and when she spoke her voice was soft. "I can give you pleasure too."

Pres watched her face as he touched her again. Her hips rose to meet his exploring fingers and the heat in her eyes turned molten. "That sounds like fun," he murmured. "We can save the real thing for another time."

"No," she said. "You don't understand.... In

the kitchen . . . In my little purse . . . There wasn't room for much, but I do have a condom."

Molly laughed at the expression on Pres's face. "Don't look so shocked," she added.

"I'm not shocked," he said. "I'm thrilled. I'm . . . confused. Do you always . . . ?"

"Carry a condom?" she asked. "No. Just . . . recently." She gazed up at him. "Are you going to go get it, or are we going to talk about it some more?"

Pres laughed, then kissed her, then disappeared down the hall.

He was back before she could blink, moving purposefully into the room, his eyes sweeping hotly across her, his quick smile not diluting the desire that seemed to radiate from him. He sat down on the bed and opened the paper wrapping of the condom, his eyes never leaving her.

Molly knew that she was looking at him just as hungrily. His tanned skin gleamed in the dim light, his rock-solid muscles shifted and flexed with his every move. He had the body of an athlete, with long, powerful-looking legs and hard-muscled shoulders and arms. He moved gracefully, confidently, at ease with his nakedness. He was beautiful.

"Your photo spread would have sold more than a million copies of *Fantasy Man* magazine," she told him.

Pres laughed, aware that she was watching him as he covered himself, her eyes following the movement of his hands. Finally, he was done, and he reached for her, but she was already next to him, kneeling on the bed, kissing his throat, his face, his lips, touching with her hands what her eyes had caressed just seconds ago.

She was ready for him, and God knows he was ready for her. But when he would have eased her back onto his pillows, she straddled his lap, impaling herself upon him with one quick, smooth movement.

Pres heard himself moan, heard Molly's voice intertwined with his. The sudden jolt of pleasure was intensified by the fact that he'd never expected her to take the lead. She pushed him back onto the bed and he thrust up harder, deeper, and she cried out again.

And then she was moving, setting a rhythm that made his blood burn. He pulled her more tightly against him, trying to tell her with the power of a kiss all that he was feeling, trying to fill her as thoroughly and completely as she filled him.

Never in a million years had he imagined she would make love to him this way. She was totally uninhibited, allowing her passion to rule her.

And what a passion it was.

She smiled as she met his eyes, and his heart damn near burst. She loved him. She *had* to love him. How could she *not* love him and make love to him so desperately, so intensely?

"I've had a couple of really hot dreams about you that were just like this," she whispered, her breath warm against his ear.

Pres couldn't talk, couldn't speak. He'd had dreams about her, too, but they hadn't come close to this incredible reality. He hadn't imagined making love could ever be this good. What he'd shared with Merrilee—or anyone else, for that matter—had never been like this.

He was out of control and mere moments from his release. He closed his eyes and buried his face in the softness of her breasts, unable to fight the onslaught of sensations, the swirl of excruciating pleasure and soul-shaking emotions that swept around and through him.

He slipped his hand between them, touching her lightly at first then harder, determined to take her with him when he went over the edge.

"Oh," she breathed. "Oh, Pres...that feels good...."

Pres made the mistake of opening his eyes. He looked up at Molly and saw her head thrown back in ecstasy, her full breasts slick with perspiration and taut with desire, and he exploded.

It was a rocket-powered trip that shot him impossibly high. He cried out, his voice raw, his throat scorched from the heat of the fireball that ripped through him and threatened to consume his very soul.

He heard Molly's answering cry of pleasure and felt her body tighten around him, pulsating, shaking with the intensity of her own release.

And then it was over. She held him tightly, as tightly as he held her. They breathed together in unison. It seemed probable that they'd remain in such perfect sync for the rest of their lives.

The rest of their lives...

Pres wanted to tell her that he loved her. He wanted to shout the words, have them reverberate throughout his bungalow and echo across the island. But he didn't dare.

It would be far too much, too soon.

FOURTEEN

MOLLY SLIPPED HER dress back on, fighting the wave of emotion that threatened to overpower her.

"Are you sure you can't stay until morning?" Preston's voice was soft, persuasive.

She wanted to stay. But she wanted to stay for longer than just the morning. She shook her head, not trusting her voice.

She heard him pull on his pants as she searched the floor for her shoes, but then remembered she'd left them on the beach.

She was a fool. What, really, had she expected?

Some kind of fairy-tale happy ending? Had she really thought that just because Pres told her about his ex-wife, and just because he took her to his private bungalow, that he'd totally open himself up to her from this time forth? Had she really thought that they would make love and as a result he'd never keep another secret from her?

That was a laugh.

Mere moments after what had to have been the most intense sexual experience of her life, he'd virtually stopped talking.

She'd teasingly told him that now that she was no longer distracted, he was going to have to tell her what his dream was—the one that he had claimed was so hokey.

He was quiet for a moment—too quiet. That was what tipped her off. He wasn't going to tell her the truth. He'd decided that it was too private for him to share with her.

Oh, he'd made up some lame substitute, something about keeping Sunrise Key as clean and unexploited as possible, fighting overdevelopment, setting up a bird sanctuary.

All of her insecurities came crashing down around her. Everything she was afraid of seemed to loom as imminent realities. Pres couldn't possibly love her, would *never* love her. Just like with Chuck, she was probably Pres's second choice. She was nothing more than a poor replacement for the ghost of Merrilee, a fictional woman who still held his heart.

She tried to tell herself that she was overreacting. She tried to tell herself that his hiding the truth really wasn't that big a deal. But it *was* a big deal. For her, the fact that he hadn't been completely honest and open with her was a *very* big deal.

So she tried to tease him. That couldn't possibly be what his dream was. She was so positive that he was going to tell her something *really* hokey, like he wanted to try to lose his image as a corporate shark and international playboy and become a kindergarten teacher—or maybe even a stay-at-home dad. She dared him to tell her the *real* truth.

Pres had laughed and insisted that he had.

But then he became so quiet, so introspective, so lost in his own world. And it was a world to which she couldn't belong if he wouldn't let her in.

And he wasn't letting her in.

It didn't seem possible that one moment she could have been so utterly euphoric, and the next plunged so deeply into despair.

She didn't say a single word, afraid if she so much as opened her mouth, her own secret would come spilling out: She was in love with him.

So Molly had closed her eyes and held tightly to him, praying that if she only waited long enough, she would hear his soft, raspy voice tell her that he loved her too. If only he loved her, that would be enough. If he loved her, she could help him learn to share himself with her. If he loved her...

But she'd heard only the silence of the night. It pressed down on her, suffocating and heavy with its accompanying disappointment.

He was clearly keeping some kind of secret from her. And whatever this secret was, it was a big one.

Pres searched the floor for his shirt and bow tie. He had to walk Molly back to the resort. As much as he felt like simply throwing on a pair of shorts and a T-shirt, it wouldn't do to look disheveled and half-dressed. True, they were supposed to be engaged, and after some of those pictures that had appeared in the papers and on TV, the entire world assumed they were sexually involved. But now that they actually were, it seemed more important than ever to preserve their privacy.

He wanted Molly to spend the night with him. He wanted to wake up tomorrow morning with her in his arms. But it wasn't going to happen—at least not until all of the attention died down.

It was probably just as good. He was trying his damnedest to slow himself down. Mother of God, when she'd teasingly suggested that his dream was to become a stay-at-home dad, he'd nearly choked. She was closer to the truth than she would have believed. But he couldn't talk about how badly he wanted to have children—not after making love for the very first time. The topic seemed a little premature. And he was trying desperately not to be impulsive. It was extremely hard. He was afraid to talk at all.

"I'm scared to death," Molly suddenly said, breaking the silence.

Pres looked up at her. She'd turned to face him. Her arms were folded tightly across her chest.

"Scared?" he repeated.

"Scared of what we've started here." She wet her lips nervously. "Of where this is going to go."

"Where do you want this to go?" he asked quietly, half hoping she wouldn't talk of commitment, and half hoping that she would.

Molly didn't seem to hear his question. She gazed down at the patterned boards of the floor. "I feel as if I'm about to do one of your skydives, only I'm not wearing a parachute." She looked up at him then, and he realized her eyes were filled with tears. "I don't know if I can do this, Pres. I don't know if I can be your lover. I thought I could, but . . . I think maybe we shouldn't see each other again for a while."

Pres was stunned. Even with all of his self-doubts and second thoughts, he'd never considered the option of simply ending whatever this was they'd started. "But you just . . . *We* just . . . You didn't think what we just did was great?"

"It was *too* great."

"There's no such thing as too great—"

"It's too high-risk."

Pres stood up, wanting to move toward her but afraid if he did she'd back away. "Are you kidding? Where's the risk? There's *no* risk at all. We're *great* together, both in bed and out."

"I'm afraid I'm going to..." She hesitated, choosing her words carefully. "I'm afraid of becoming too attached. To you."

Pres sat down again. He, too, selected his words. "Do you think that's possible? You think you might...become too attached. To me?"

Again, she didn't answer his question. "I think I need some time to figure out—"

"Because I think there's a real possibility that I could become too attached to you." God, was that the most ass-backward declaration of love that had ever been made in the world or what?

Molly stared at him, her eyes wide. She shook her head, the way a pitcher might shake off a catcher's signal for a pitch. "Don't," she said. "I don't want you to. Because to tell you the truth, I need more than you can give me, Pres."

Silence crackled around them as Pres gazed at her in astonishment.

God, *that* hurt. Her soft words had knocked some of the air out of him, and he had to look away and catch his breath. Except his stomach and lungs felt so numb, he was certain he'd never catch his breath again. She needed more than he could give her? What the hell did that mean? She couldn't possibly be talking about sex, because what they had just shared was off the scale. Wasn't it?

"Oh," he finally said. "I didn't...I don't..." He gave up trying to hide his bewilderment. "I don't understand."

"I need more than sexual intimacy," Molly said softly. "I want openness and honesty and the truth—*all* the time. I think you're far too private a person to be able to give me that."

"But I told you things I've never told *anyone*." He ran his hand back through his hair. "I brought you *here*...."

"After we made love, you didn't say anything—"

Pres laughed, a hot burst of frustration. "Because after what we did, I was only semiconscious. Mother of God, Molly—"

"I need to know how you're feeling, *what* you're feeling! Chuck never gave me that, and I'm not going to fall into that same emotional trap."

"I'm not Chuck!"

She moved toward him, imploringly. "Then talk to me!"

What could he say to her? What could he tell her? That he was scared to death because of the strength and depth of these emotions he was feeling? Was he supposed to tell her that he'd felt this exact same way with Merrilee, and because of that he needed to back away, keep some distance from Molly? Was he supposed to say that he didn't trust his own emotions, didn't quite believe that what he was feeling was truly real?

Was he supposed to tell her that if Merrilee hadn't come first, he'd probably be down on his knees right this moment, begging Molly to be his wife? How could he possibly tell her that?

"There are some things I just can't tell you," he said tightly.

She nodded. "I know. Like I said, you can't give me what I need."

He stood up, reaching for her. "Can't you give me some time to figure all this out?"

Molly backed away. "Pres, I'm sorry. I can't take that kind of a chance."

She was out the door so fast, Pres couldn't stop her. He wasn't even sure he wanted to stop her.

But he did follow her, trailing along a distance behind her as she hurried down the beach toward the resort.

He followed her until he saw that she was safely inside the main building, and then he turned and automatically walked home.

His bungalow smelled like Molly's sweet perfume. And sitting right in the middle of his kitchen table was the sapphire engagement ring he'd given to her.

It wasn't an engagement ring. They'd never really been engaged.

So why the hell did seeing it there make him feel as if his heart had been ripped from his chest?

Pres went into the kitchen and took that last pack of cigarettes from the drawer. He removed the cellophane wrapper and opened the box. He couldn't find any damn matches, so he lit it directly from one of the stove's gas burners and drew a deep breath in.

He blew the smoke out, praying it would erase the sweet scent that Molly had left behind.

But all it did was leave a bitter taste in his mouth.

The morning sun was much too bright.

Molly put her sunglasses on as she drove Zander to school.

He was late. She had overslept in the quiet peacefulness of the hotel suite, without the roofers to wake her up at the crack of dawn. She'd returned to the resort the night before, fully intending to take Zander and go home. But Zander had been sound asleep, and the thought of carrying the gangly ten-year-old all the way up to his bedroom in the Kirk Estate was daunting.

So she'd stayed.

And overslept.

"I don't have anything to write a note on," she told him as she pulled into the school parking lot. "So I'll walk you in, okay?"

Zander was clutching his backpack. "Do I *have* to go to school today? Since I'm already late, can't I just stay home?"

"Don't you want to go?" Molly asked. Zander loved school—or at least he had before. "Is your new school okay?"

He wouldn't meet her eyes. "It's...new, I guess."

She turned off the engine and turned to face him. "Zander, is something wrong at school? You haven't talked about it that much. Is something going on that I should know about?"

He opened the car door and started to climb out. "Is it okay if we don't talk about it right now? You're not in the best mood...."

"Is whatever you're going to tell me going to put me in an even *worse* mood?" Molly got out and looked at him over the top of the car.

"It might."

"Is whatever you're going to tell me something that's dangerous, or something that could hurt you or make you sick?"

Zander shook his head. "No."

"Then will you promise to tell me right after you get home from school?"

"I promise."

Molly started toward the school entrance, giving Zander a quick hug around the shoulders. "Then okay."

Zander hugged her back. "Mom, you're so cool."

She had to smile.

"You're as cool as Pres," he added.

Her smile faded. Pres Seaholm. She didn't want to think about him, but she'd thought of no one and nothing else from the moment she'd awakened. And last night she'd dreamed about him endlessly.

She didn't want to love him the way that she did. She didn't want to take that kind of emotional risk. And maybe if she could just keep away from him, her feelings wouldn't grow any stronger. Maybe if she didn't see him all the time, her feelings would start to fade.

But it was damned hard to avoid him when he invaded her every thought.

She pulled open the door. As she and Zander stepped into the air-conditioned coolness of the school, she tried to banish Pres from her mind.

The school's main office was directly to the right of the entrance. Kim Kavanaugh, the principal, came out as they approached, her sixteen-month-old daughter on her hip.

Mrs. Kavanaugh greeted Zander brightly. "Oh, great, you made it. We're having an assembly this afternoon—a string quartet from Sarasota is going to play for the school. I was afraid you were going to miss it." She turned to Molly. "And I'm glad you're here too. I've spent the past two hours calling the fifth- and sixth-grade parents—Mr. Towne handed in his resignation this morning. As of today, he's gone."

Zander dropped his backpack. "Mr. Towne did *what*? He's *what*?"

"Gone," Mrs. Kavanaugh repeated. "He gave his resignation—that means he quit. Just like that. Can you believe it?"

Zander started to laugh. "Yeah," he said. "Yeah, I can believe it. Pres is the *best*!" He did a little dance in a circle in the hall. "Yes! Yes, yes, *yes*!"

Molly caught his arm. "Zander, what's going on?"

"Yesterday I told Pres all about how mean Mr. Towne was, and now Mr. Towne is gone!" Quickly, and nearly all in one breath, Zander recounted everything about Mr. Towne that he'd told Pres the evening before.

Kim Kavanaugh was livid. "The nerve of that man!" she exclaimed. "Stanley Towne had no right—*no right*—to be a teacher. The school board had been trying to get rid of him for years. But he had tenure and we couldn't afford to pay him the amount he was demanding for an early retirement."

Molly was numb. "Zander, why didn't you tell me any of this?" Her son had told Pres, but he hadn't told her.

He gazed at her solemnly from behind his glasses. "I didn't want you to break Mr. Towne's nose."

"I wouldn't have broken his nose! I would have been very, very angry, yes, but..." Molly pulled Zander into her arms and gave him a hug. "Please, don't ever not tell me something like this again."

"I won't," he promised. He looked up at her. "Do you think Pres really took his diving spear and went after Mr. Towne?"

"What?"

"He said he oughta—"

"Zander, we don't even know that Pres had anything to do with Mr. Towne leaving." But even as she spoke the words she knew they were ridiculous. Of course Pres had done something. He'd no doubt paid the man off, made it worth Towne's while to leave.

"Who's gonna teach my class?" Zander asked Mrs. Kavanaugh.

The principal shifted her baby to her other hip. "Actually, Mr. Young is going to be your substitute teacher—until we find a permanent replacement." She looked up at Molly. "You know Hayden Young, right? Tall, long blond hair? Of course you do—he's Zander's speech teacher, right?"

"He's so cool," Zander exclaimed. Coolness in Sunrise Key was apparently contagious. "Is he here now?"

Mrs. Kavanaugh nodded.

Zander was poised, quivering, eager to be on his way to his classroom. "Can I—*may* I go?"

Mrs. Kavanaugh nodded again. "Please don't run, Zander," she called after him. "We'll be looking to hire someone with special-education experience to replace Mr. Towne," she told Molly. "Although I have this secret dream of talking Hayden Young into taking the job on a permanent basis."

"I had no idea," Molly murmured, hardly hearing the other woman. "Zander didn't say a word. But I should have known. It took him so long to get ready for school these past few mornings. I should have guessed that something wasn't right." She glanced at Kim Kavanaugh, lowering her voice. "Did Mr. Towne give you a reason for his leaving? I mean, he broke his contract, right? Surely he gave you some excuse."

"He told me only that he'd suddenly come into a great deal of money, and that he was willing to accept the school board's last offer for early retirement on the condition he would be able to leave immediately. As in today. Do you think . . ."

"That Preston Seaholm was behind that 'great deal of money'?" Molly nodded grimly. "There's not a doubt in my mind."

She turned to go, but Kim Kavanaugh's soft words stopped her.

"He must love you and Zander very much."

Love. Yeah, right.

Pres didn't know how to share his love. He didn't seem to be able to share anything but his money.

FIFTEEN

PRES HAD A head-on collision with Molly at the door to Millie's Market. She was going in and he was coming out.

He gazed down at her from behind his dark glasses. She didn't look happy. In fact, she looked downright *un*happy. Well, hell, that made two of them.

"I was just on my way over to your place," he said.

"I just came from *your* place." She was unable to keep from glancing at the pack of cigarettes in his hand. "I want to talk to you. About Stanley Towne?"

He looked around, searching for news cameras and stray photographers. There were none in sight. "Let's walk."

"Did you pay off Zander's teacher so that he'd quit?"

Pres didn't answer right away. He peeled the cellophane wrapper from the pack and threw it into a trash barrel. Seeing Molly again made his craving for cigarettes fade to almost nothing. Instead, he desperately craved *her*. It was a deeper, stronger, more powerful need, and his entire chest hurt from wanting her. He put a cigarette in his mouth instead. "Mind if I smoke?"

"Yes."

"But we're outside...."

"You asked, and yes, I do mind. I don't want you to smoke, all right?"

She was upset, and she wasn't the only one. Pres broke the cigarette in two, turned back to the trash barrel, and threw it in. He slammed the entire rest of the pack in after it.

Molly was astonished. Cool, imperturbable Preston Seaholm had actually lost his temper. As she watched he gripped the edge of a pay-phone booth, as if trying to cool down. But when he turned back to her, his mouth was still grimly set.

"I can't believe after what we shared last night, you don't want to make even the *smallest* attempt to make it work between us," he said.

"Did you or did you not give Stanley Towne money?"

Pres yanked off his sunglasses and his eyes looked stormy. "Yes, I did. I went to see him this morning. I paid him off so that he'd leave town. So yes, I'm guilty of using my money to help you and Zander. No, I'm not trying to *buy* you. No, I didn't think doing this would bring you running back to me, arms open wide. I did it because I wanted to. What's the use in having money if you can't spend it the way you want to?"

"It feels so wrong to me," Molly said hotly. "Every time I turn around, there you are, ready to spend another small fortune on Zander and me. It leaves a bad taste in my mouth. It makes me start to doubt my own reasons for wanting to be with you—I mean, face it, my life would be so much easier if I took that grant. Or if I became your lover, and just let you pay for everything."

Pres stared at her, trying to understand, wanting to understand so that he could figure out a way to persuade her that she was wrong.

"So how do you know that the reason you think you *don't* want to be with me isn't because you're afraid of being influenced by my money?" he finally asked.

Molly gazed back at him. She was afraid of many things when it came to Preston Seaholm, but that wasn't one of them. "That's not why I... can't be with you."

Pres crossed the sidewalk and sat down on the bench in the shade of the florist's awning. "That's right. I almost forgot. You think I'm too much like what's-his-name."

Molly sat down tiredly next to him. "I can't willingly enter a relationship that seems so much like one that didn't work. You're the same kind of person Chuck was—so careful of your privacy. I don't want to be in a relationship where I have to guess what my lover is thinking."

Pres put his head in his hands. "Well, you'll never guess in a million years what I'm thinking right now." He took a deep breath, glancing at her out of the corner of his eyes. "We need to get married."

"Excuse me?"

He leaned back on the bench, long legs stretched out in front of him as he ran both hands through his hair and then down his face. "Somehow the rumor got started that we're getting married on Saturday. Instead of the camera teams going away, the entertainment news programs are sending more equipment down to Sunrise Key to cover what's promising to be the wedding of the year."

Molly had to laugh, giddy with disbelief. But she knew Pres wasn't kidding—why would he kid about something like that?

"I called a friend of mine who works for a major public-relations firm up in New York City," Pres continued. "I asked him the best way to handle this, and he recommended that we give them what they want. And pray that this time it works."

"Would you care for something from the dessert cart, madam?"

"Mom? Yo. Mom!"

Molly blinked and focused on Zander's face. He pointed behind her, and she looked over her shoulder to see a tuxedo-clad waiter standing there, dessert cart at the ready.

"No thanks," she murmured. She glanced to her right, where Preston was sitting quietly. He'd said no more than a few sentences all night. It was her birthday, *and* it was the night before her so-called wedding. It would have been considered odd if she and Pres hadn't appeared out together. She'd thought it would be less awkward, bringing Zander along with them to dinner, but now she wasn't so sure it had helped.

It was hard to sit mere inches away from a man she was trying her damnedest not to love. She needed to be farther than six inches from him if she wanted to forget about his smile, his laughter, his incredible, electricity-filled touch.

Instead, she'd spent the past few days in constant contact with Pres. And when she wasn't with him, she was being fitted for a wedding gown.

Tomorrow she was pretending to marry a man

whom she would have married for real in a heart-beat, if he only would tell her that he loved her.

"So are you guys going on a honeymoon?" Zander asked, oblivious to the strained silence.

"Zander, it's just a pretend wedding...."

"But you want people to *think* it's real," he said. "How are you going to make people think it's real if you don't go on a honeymoon?"

Molly glanced up to find Pres watching her. He smiled very slightly, sadly, and her heart felt squeezed.

"Maybe we should take a short trip." He took a sip of his coffee. "We could take Zander with us. Where would you want to go, Z?"

Her son's eyes lit up. "I'd want to go to see your shipwreck." He concentrated hard to pronounce all of the *s*'s. "To that place where your friend's salvage company is digging it back out of the sand."

"St. John," Pres said. He looked at Molly. "That's not a bad idea, actually. I could do some diving, and you and Zander could hang out on the beach, or take a boat over to St. Thomas for shopping." He lowered his voice even further.

"You wouldn't have to spend much time with me at all."

Zander was radiating excitement. "Pres showed me pictures of St. John, Mom. It's *so* pretty. And the water's so clear, you can see all kinds of tropical fish. Hey! Pres can start teaching me to snorkel while we're there! Remember, Pres, you promised you'd teach me to snorkel."

Molly turned to Pres in amazement. "You *promised* him...?"

Pres dug some money out of his pocket. "Hey, Z, do me a favor, and go ask the bandleader to play 'Stardust' for your mom, okay? You need to go over there and wait until they finish playing, all right?" He handed the boy several dollar bills. "Put that in that giant glass on top of the piano. That's their tip."

"What about *my* tip?"

"Zander!" Molly hissed.

"I was kidding! It was a joke!"

"Go." Both Pres and Molly spoke in unison.

Zander was barely away from the table before they turned to face each other like a pair of wary boxers.

Pres spoke first. "There's nothing dangerous about learning to snorkel."

"But if he learns to snorkel, he'll expect to be able to learn to dive when he's old enough." Molly shook her head. "And that *is* too dangerous. I'm not going to let him do it."

Pres was silent for a moment. "You don't know why he wants to learn to dive, do you?"

"He wants to dive because you do, because you're his hero."

"No, that's not why." Pres looked across the room, to where Zander was standing off to the one side, watching the band. "He wants to dive because underwater, he won't be any different from anyone else. Nobody can hear underwater. It's virtually silent down there."

Pres looked back at Molly, watching her emotions play across her face.

"Think about it," he continued. "His hearing loss, his deafness, it won't matter at all when he's underwater. That's why the kid wants to dive. For the first time in his life he wouldn't be at a disadvantage. He has the right to experience that, don't you think?"

Molly was silent, her blue eyes filled with realization and tears.

Pres went on. "And divers communicate through a very basic, very rough form of sign language. Knowing ASL would put Zander at a tremendous advantage."

Across the room, the band had stopped playing. "Excuse me." A small voice spoke into the bandleader's microphone. It was Zander. He was actually up on the stage, looking out at them. "I want to tell my mom happy birthday. She doesn't like cake, and there's no candle for her to blow out, but I hope she gets her wish anyway."

Behind him the band began to play, and Zander began to sing the old familiar birthday song.

Pres had never really heard the boy sing before.

"He's amazing," he murmured, glancing at Molly. Zander's voice was pure and clear, a sweet boy soprano that faltered only slightly on the high notes.

Molly covered her mouth with one hand and laughed as Zander signed "I love you" to her then took an exaggerated bow. He turned to talk to the bandleader again.

"He *is* amazing," she said.

"Let him learn to scuba-dive."

"Oh, Lord, it's so dangerous! How could I let him?"

"How could you not?" Pres covered her hand with his. "You know, some things are worth the risk. For Zander, this is definitely worth it."

Molly leaned toward him. "Did he actually say all this to you?"

"More or less." He smiled. "Less, actually. I mean, the kid's ten, right? All he really knows is that he wants to learn to dive really bad. I figured out the why part from listening to him talk—the things he said, how he said it."

"You're very perceptive, aren't you?"

He gazed at her levelly. "Not all of communicating is talking. Knowing how to listen is important too."

Molly was caught in the ocean depths of his eyes.

"Come on. Let Zander learn to dive," he murmured.

Molly hesitated only briefly before she nodded, turning her hand over so that their fingers were laced together. "Promise you'll be the one to teach him?"

He nodded. "I promise."

"And you'll make sure he's safe?"

Pres nodded. "Molly, you know that I'll take care of your son." He paused, looking down at their hands. "If you can trust me to keep Zander safe, you can trust me enough to know that I'd never intentionally hurt you. I don't want to stay away from you. I want to be your lover."

She tried to pull her hand away. "Pres—"

He leaned forward, refusing to let her go. "Come on, Molly. Take a risk. I know I'm not exactly what you're looking for, but you can spend your entire life looking for perfection, afraid to make a mistake and—"

He broke off, a strange expression on his face, hardly noticing when her hand slipped free. "Afraid to make a mistake." He frowned. "Maybe even afraid to make the same mistake twice..."

And then Zander came bounding back to the table.

Molly hugged her son and thanked him for his song, aware that Pres was watching her, aware of a strange light in his eyes.

She gathered her purse up from the table. "I

think it's time to go. We all have to be up early in the morning...."

Pres stood up, still oddly preoccupied. "I'll drive you home."

Molly paced.

It was two o'clock in the morning, and she couldn't sleep.

It was remarkable. She was more nervous about tomorrow's make-believe wedding than she'd been about her real wedding more than ten years ago.

Of course, she'd had the advantage of being young and foolish back then.

Ten years later she was only foolish. How could she have even considered taking part in this sham? How on earth was she going to be able to walk down that aisle and repeat those wedding vows while gazing into Preston's eyes?

Take a risk. Pres's words echoed over and over in her mind. *Take a risk.*

Life was full of risks. Every time she got behind the steering wheel of her car, she was taking a risk. Heck, every time she got out of bed in the morning, every time she drew in another breath of air, she was taking a risk.

Talk about risks. She'd read in the paper about a woman who was so cautious, she refused to leave her house. And an airplane crashed into it.

She was a lot like that woman. She'd been content to stay in her own little isolated world, carefully distanced from romance, and then, *wham-o*, Pres Seaholm had crashed into her life.

The truth was, she loved him and wanted to be with him.

The truth was, she *could* wind up in exactly the same situation she'd been in with Chuck.

That was indeed a risk.

But if she simply did nothing, if she continued to turn her back on her emotions, if she let Pres slip away, well, that was a risk of an entirely different kind. She was risking what could very well turn out to be her one chance at finding happiness.

Pres wanted to be with her. He'd made that more than clear. And maybe, just maybe, with a little time, he might fall in love with her too.

But that wasn't going to happen unless she took a risk.

Preston paced.

It was nearly eleven o'clock in the morning, and the small room off the front of the Congregational church was airless and much too warm. He could feel sweat starting to drip down the back of his tuxedo shirt.

He could hear the sounds of helicopters circling overhead, poised and ready to get aerial footage of the Most Eligible Bachelor of the Year and his bride leaving the church, newly married.

Or so the world would think.

The door opened and Dominic stuck his head inside.

"Molly's arrived," he said. "She's in the back of the church. You should go out to the altar soon and get this show on the road, or she's going to be blinded from all those flashbulbs going off in her face."

Pres nodded. Get this show on the road. He ran a comb through his hair one last time, adjusted his bow tie in the mirror, and taking a deep breath, stepped out into the church.

It wasn't a big church, and it was jammed full

of news cameras and reporters, curious spectators, and even some friends. And right now they were all staring directly at him.

"It's not real," Dominic murmured into Pres's ear. "Just keep telling yourself that it's not real."

But that was the problem. It wasn't real. "I can't do this." Pres turned to look at Dom.

"Whoa." Dom put a reassuring hand on his friend's shoulder. "Just take a couple of nice, deep breaths and—"

The organist began to play the notes of the bridal processional. There was a flurry of movement at the back of the church as the doors opened. Then Molly appeared in the doorway, dressed in an ornate white gown, a light veil over her face. She looked incredible, and Pres felt his heart turn a slow somersault in his chest. But this wasn't real. This was only make-believe. And that wasn't good enough.

"I can't do this," he said again, and breaking free from Dom's grasp, he headed quickly down the aisle, toward Molly.

There was a murmur of surprise from the crowd, mirrored by the look on Molly's face.

"Excuse us for a minute," Pres said to the cameras, and shut the doors tightly behind him.

"Pres, what are you doing . . . ?"

He grabbed Molly's hand and tugged her toward the stairs that led down to the church vestry. It wasn't until they were in the tiled room with the door shut behind them that Pres spoke.

"I'm sorry, but I just can't do this."

She pushed the veil back, off of her face. "But if your friend from that New York PR agency is right, once we do this, we'll be left alone."

"I can't pretend to marry you," he told her. "I can't stand there and say those words."

"It's just a role we have to play. An act. That's what you told me, remember? You said it's just something that we have to do. It's not real."

"But that's just it." He started to pace again, but stopped himself. "Molly, I want it to be real."

She was staring at him as if he were spouting gibberish.

"I can't pretend to marry you, because I *want* to marry you."

Her eyes were wide, her lips slightly parted in an expression of sheer astonishment. Whatever she'd expected him to say, it wasn't this.

"I've wanted to marry you nearly from the start," he continued, "but I was so busy trying not to make the same damned mistake with you that I made with Merrilee that I nearly blew it. I was trying to take my time, trying not to be impulsive, trying to keep history from repeating itself. But the fact is, you're not Merrilee. You're not Merrilee, and I'm not Chuck, and we could really make this thing between us work. I know there are no guarantees, but just the same, it has to be worth the risk."

It had come to him like a lightning bolt the night before. He had been urging Molly to take a risk, not to be weighed down by mistakes she'd made in the past, when it suddenly occurred to him that he could use a healthy dose of his own advice.

So much of his relationship with Molly had reminded him of his first marriage. So many things were similar, including his desire to establish a permanent relationship after only a very short amount of time. But at the same time so much was different. Molly wasn't Merrilee.

"I wanted to ask you to marry me the night we

made love," he told her. "And I should have. I should have trusted myself. Instead I got spooked and tried to figure it all out. And of course, I couldn't. I was afraid if I opened my mouth I'd tell you that I loved you and I'd beg you to marry me. I thought that was the wrong thing to do, but I know now it wasn't. It was right. It *is* right."

Molly was still silent, just watching him, so Pres took a deep breath and kept going. "I know I'm... less than adequate when it comes to opening up about the way I feel, but if you'll give me a chance, and maybe a little help, I swear to God above, I'll try...."

She laughed, a short, sharp sound, rather like a hiccup. "You seem to be doing just fine today."

He took her hand. "Marry me, Molly. For real."

"You love me?" There were tears in her eyes. "You really love me?"

"More than I'll ever be able to tell you."

Molly couldn't speak. She turned away, and Pres felt a wave of panic. She'd turned away even though he'd told her everything he possibly could and—

"I didn't tell you the truth about that dream of mine," he said. "You know, the really hokey one?"

She turned back to look at him. "I know."

This time Pres didn't hesitate. "I want kids. I want to be a dad. A real, round-the-clock, hands-on dad."

Molly couldn't believe what she was hearing. She laughed, but he held up his hand.

"There's more. I want to have a whole pack of kids," he told her, "and be their little-league coach and teach them to dive and fish and sail and read, and to be there for them for the rest of their lives."

His dream was to have children. Who would've thought . . . ?

"I hadn't thought about it in a while," Pres admitted, "but these past few weeks, hanging out with Zander . . . It felt good, Molly. It reminded me of what I've always wanted."

"Why didn't you tell me?" She took his hands. "That night . . . you should have told me the truth. . . ."

"I couldn't," he said simply. "How could I talk about having kids with you? Number one, I was afraid of scaring you off. Number two, I was afraid I'd suddenly blurt out a marriage proposal. I was afraid if I started talking I might tell you that while we were making love I was wishing we could have been making a baby. I thought that talking about babies might've been a rather strong hint that I'd already started thinking in terms of forever."

Forever.

"Say something," he said. He was oddly, sweetly nervous.

"I don't know what to say."

"Say you'll marry me. Say that you and Zander and I, we can become a family. Say you love me, too, even though I'm not perfect. . . ."

There was a knock on the door. "Everything okay in there?" Dominic's voice called out.

Pres looked at Molly. "Is everything okay in here?"

She felt off balance and giddy, light-headed and dizzy. But everything was more okay than it had been in a long, long, *long* time. "Yes," she called out. "Everything's okay. And yes, I'll marry you," she added much more softly.

Pres kissed her, a slow, deep kiss that promised her that forever.

"Hey," Dominic said, slipping in through the door. "You're not supposed to do that until after the pastor says you can."

The wedding. They were supposed to be up in that church right now, exchanging make-believe wedding vows.

"Sorry to interrupt, Pres," Dom continued, "but Ben Sullivan's here and he's insisting that he gets a chance to talk to you before the ceremony starts."

The door opened and a sandy-haired man in a cowboy hat poked his head into the room.

"What's up, Ben?" Pres asked. "Come on in and meet Molly Cassidy. Molly, Ben's my attorney."

"Thank heavens I got here in time." Ben closed the door behind him, taking off his hat as he came into the room. "Prenups," he said. "I know this is all a sham, but the fact that this is a church, and the pastor is a real man of God, gives me the heebie-jeebies. I can't let you do this without signing a prenuptial agreement." He opened his briefcase and took several documents out.

But Pres was already shaking his head. "The only agreement I need drawn up is a document stating the Kirk Estate is going to remain in Molly's name only. Ben, can you do that for me right away?"

Ben Sullivan blinked. "But..."

Pres turned to Dominic. "I need the jet ready to go. Please, do me a favor and tell the pilot to file a flight plan to Las Vegas? Molly and I are getting married."

"Today?" Molly laughed in disbelief.

He kissed her again. "We'll go upstairs and have a practice run, then go do the real thing. We have to go to Vegas, or wait for the marriage license. I say Vegas and I say today. What do you say?"

Yes. She wanted to say yes. "I need to talk to Zander first...."

Dominic headed for the door. "I'll get the kid."

"He's going to be all for this," Pres told her. "He's wanted you and me to get together right from the start."

"I'll get right to work on that document," Ben said, opening the door. "Have Dominic call me with your flight plans, and I'll bring it over to the airport—you can sign it there. Although as your attorney, I have to advise you to negotiate a prenuptial agreement with—"

"Thank you, Ben, you've done your job," Pres interrupted. "I'll consider myself advised and—"

"I want to sign a prenup," Molly interjected. She gazed at Pres. "I don't want your money. Lord, this is all happening so fast...."

"The money is part of who I am," he said quietly. "It's kind of a package deal."

"I don't want there to be any confusion," she said just as quietly. "Or outside speculation. There are lots of people watching us right now, Pres. I want them to know that I'm marrying you because I love you."

Pres nodded, turning abruptly to Ben. "Bring both agreements."

Ben went out the door just as Zander barreled inside. "Mom! Dom told me you and Pres were *really* gonna get married! That is *so cool*!"

Pres looked at Molly and smiled. "I think that's a stamp of approval."

She hugged Zander as she smiled back at Pres.

"Let's do it," he said. "One time for the cameras, and one time for ourselves."

"Both times for ourselves," Molly corrected him. "Just think of all the great wedding photos we're going to have."

Pres laughed. And kissed the bride.

EPILOGUE

MOLLY PUSHED the dinghy away from the side of the yacht, setting the oars in the oarlocks. She started to row with smooth, sure movements.

"Don't stand up," she gently warned Jeremiah, who sat facing her in the stern of the boat.

Her two-year-old son wore a bright yellow life vest—but only because he wasn't allowed to be on the boat without one. Like his father, he loved the water. And like his father, he was fearless.

Jeremiah's reddish-gold hair reflected the rays of the warm Caribbean sun as he searched the surface of the azure water for the telltale bubbles that would mark Preston and Zander's location. When he spotted them, he stood up excitedly.

"There Zander!" he cried, nearly leaping over the side of the little boat. "There Daddy! Ina water! Ina water!"

Molly grabbed hold of Jeremiah's sturdy little body, and he gave her a quick, excited hug. "There Zander!" he said again. "Cooba divin' 'n a mask 'n fwippers!"

Jeremiah pulled away from Molly and sat with a thud on the bottom of the boat to pull on his own flippers.

Sure enough, Zander broke the surface some distance away. He saw the dinghy almost immediately, and touched the top of his head twice—the scuba diver's signal that everything was okay. Pres was right behind him.

Jeremiah pulled himself up and immediately began signing furiously to Zander. "Wanna swim to Zander!" His words echoed the movements of his hands. "Wanna swim ina water like Zander!"

Zander lifted his hands and signed back to his little brother, telling him to swim to the yacht. He knew he had to get his tank and diving gear off before he could play with the toddler.

"Mommy, Mommy," Jeremiah singsonged. "Wanna swim ina water! Hi, Daddy! Hi, Daddy!"

"Hey, fish-kid." Pres held on to the side of the dinghy as he slipped off his mask and smiled up at Molly and their son.

"What's the magic word?" Molly asked Jeremiah.

"Pwease! Pwease!"

"No climbing on Zander until he gets his gear off," Molly reminded the little boy.

With a splash, Jeremiah was over the side and swimming like a fish back toward the yacht.

"Morning, sleepyhead." Pres lifted himself up and Molly leaned down for a kiss.

His lips were cool and soft. She kissed him again, lingering this time.

"Hmmm," Pres said, his eyes a familiar shade of heated green. "Maybe I should've stayed in bed with you this morning."

"You promised Z you'd dive with him at the crack of dawn."

"I did. I thought you did too."

Molly smiled. "I only said maybe. The crack of dawn and I aren't getting along too well these days."

Back at the yacht, Randy and Dave, two of Pres's crew, had helped Zander out of his diving gear. With a splash, Zander went back into the water where Jeremiah was still paddling around.

"We didn't stay down for long, thinking you might want to dive with me this afternoon." Pres grinned at the sound of his small son's excited squealing. "Zander even volunteered to baby-sit."

But Molly shook her head. "I'm not going to do any diving this trip," she told her husband. "In fact, I think it's going to be at *least* another eight months before I dive again."

She watched the realization spread across Pres's face.

"Really?" he breathed.

"I did a home pregnancy test this morning. We're going to have another baby." She couldn't help but laugh at the look on his face.

But the wonder and awe in his eyes was instantly replaced by concern. "But you said you wanted to wait until after you finished the revisions on your book and—"

Molly kissed Pres again. "I'll get the work done

somehow." She smiled at him. "You can take Jeremiah into work with you more often."

"I will. Zander too." Pres touched the side of her face. "God, I love you, Mol."

"Sometimes the best things in life arrive unexpectedly," Molly said softly, looking down into the warm green eyes of one of the best things that had ever arrived unexpectedly into her life.

"Is it too soon to tell the kids?" Pres asked, his face alight with excitement.

Molly shook her head no.

Pres swam for the yacht, pulling the dinghy along behind him. "Hey, guys! Hey, Zander! Yo, Jerry! The word for the day is *baby*!"

ABOUT THE AUTHOR

Since her explosion onto the publishing scene more than ten years ago, SUZANNE BROCK-MANN has written over forty books and is now widely recognized as one of the leading voices in romantic suspense. Her work has earned her re-peated appearances on the *USA Today* and *New York Times* bestseller lists, as well as numerous awards, including the Romance Writers of Amer-ica's #1 Favorite Book for the Year three years running—in 2000, 2001, and 2002—two RITA awards, and many *Romantic Times* Reviewer's Choice Awards. Suzanne lives west of Boston with her husband, Dell author Ed Gaffney. Visit her website at www.SuzanneBrockmann.com.

ABOUT THE AUTHOR